HARDENED HEARTS

UNNERVING

HARDENED HEARTS

EDITED BY EDDIE GENEROUS

HARDENED HEARTS

HARDENED HEARTS

HARDENED HEARTS

FOREWORD

JAMES NEWMAN

"Love is a fire. But whether it is going to warm your hearth or burn down your house, you can never tell."
— Joan Crawford

"Love is not blind. Love is a cannibal with extremely acute vision. Love is insectile; it is always hungry."
— Stephen King, *Christine*

Love hurts. Love bites. Love's a bitch. Love is a battlefield.

I hate myself for loving you.

Love isn't always pretty, is it? In fact, it can be downright scary, which is why for every catchy-but-disgustingly-sappy song with a title like *Love Will Keep Us Together* there's one that strongly begs to differ: *Love Will Tear Us Apart*.

There's a good reason why LOVE is a four-letter word.

Because LOVE can be scary as fuck, man.

According to science-fiction/fantasy author Ursula K. LeGuin, "A profound love between two people involves (the) power and chance of doing profound hurt."

Truer words were never written.

When two people fall in love, they enter into a covenant. A part of each person's heart is now shared with another, and with that arrangement comes a promise that his or her partner's hopes, fears, and physical and mental welfare is more important than his or her own.

That's a lot to live up to, right? Sometimes we try but fail. Most of us have known at some point what it feels like when a relationship doesn't work out, if by no fault of our own. When love goes bad—whether it's because two people simply drifted apart over time, or infidelity crept in like a burglar in the middle of the night, or perhaps that old sonofabitch the Grim Reaper stepped in to cut things short with his scythe—it's the worst feeling in the world. Takes a while to get over it. Sometimes you never do, depending on the situation.

My favorite kind of horror has always come from those books and movies that aren't just about zombies munching on brains or giant blobs from outer space devouring everything in their path. Granted, I adore that stuff too, but the stories that resonate the most—as with any art, no matter the medium or genre—are those that have something to say about the human condition. Stephen King was the author who shaped me more than any other, making me the writer I am today, and it's his fourteenth novel, *Christine*, that remains my favorite thirty years after I read it for the first time. Why? Because it's more than just some silly yarn about a demonic car that runs bullies down in the street. *Christine* is a tragic love story about a young outcast who falls in love with the one girl—in this case, a 1958 Plymouth Fury—who will never break his heart as long as he is loyal in return. But with that love comes sacrifice, as poor Arnie Cunningham's friends and family take a backseat (if you'll excuse the pun) to his obsession with the titular car. Another King novel that applies here is *Pet Sematary*, in which a father's love for his late son impedes his ability to ponder the consequences of his actions. Love changes those who fall beneath its spell, and more often than not, it cripples all reason.

The best horror stories leave audiences not only with their forearms prickled with goosebumps but perhaps a tad teary-eyed too when all is said and done. Characters we care about are imperative in good storytelling, but there's twice as much at stake for two people we wish to see attain their "happily ever after." In the horror genre that doesn't always happen. Effective horror must leave us damaged in some way, I believe, because we wish for so much more for these characters even as we know the power of love isn't enough to save them. A few examples that immediately come to mind: *Rosemary's Baby* (about a mother's affection for her unborn child, and her battle with those she thinks wish to harm it) . . . David Cronenberg's *The Fly* (a heartbreaking allegory about watching a loved one slowly eaten alive by a chronic disease) . . . and, more recently, *Honeymoon* (do we ever really know the person with whom we share our most intimate, vulnerable moments?). I would be remiss if I didn't include as well the classic tale of King Kong and Ann Darrow. If you can look past the, erm, bestiality, what is *King Kong* if not a heart-wrenching story of two beautiful souls fighting to survive in a world that wants to tear them apart?

The stories in *Hardened Hearts* are about love that hurts. They are tales of forbidden love, and love that's on borrowed time. They are stories about sexual love and love between star-crossed romantics, but also included here are stories of a guilt-ridden father's love for his little girl, obsessions with inanimate objects, and even one woman's unnatural, and shared, love for a spider (!).

Love is strange, like the Everly Brothers sang way back in 1965, but once you've got it you never wanna quit.

And, as each entry in this fine anthology proves, there's nothing on Earth that's more terrifying.

HARDENED HEARTS

40 WAYS TO LEAVE YOUR MONSTER LOVER

GWENDOLYN KISTE

Just run. Run, and never look back.

Don't become his lover in the first place.

That would be the best way out, not that you ever take the easy escape. Girls who don't venture deeper into the woods aren't very interesting, are they? You can't become the heroine of your own story until you creep into the darkness and confront the wolf.

But the first thing you see when you meet him isn't a wolf. It's a glittering green bottle of gin, the top-shelf variety. You're standing alone at a party, fidgeting in a brown satin dress you've had since high school. Three of your friends from the sociology department brought you here, but they abandoned you as soon as the music was turned up loud enough to drown out your cries of protest. They didn't want you here in the first place. You were the pity invite.

As you press yourself against the wall, a shadow passes over your face, and you glance up, your heart already quickening. First, you see the gin label with its fancy cursive letters. Then your gaze slides up the glass neck of the bottle to the hand that's holding it, a hand with a circle of gold around the ring finger. That alone should stop you. It doesn't. Your eyes flick up and you see his face, already smiling into yours.

His is not a terrible face as far as faces go, but it's not particularly striking either. He's older than you, a fringe of gray over his dark eyes. You could probably do better than him, could probably find someone closer to your own age, someone more like you. But that would take work and you're not always good at working for things. That's why you're a permanent grad student with a questionable GPA and even more questionable taste in friends.

As he keeps smiling at you, don't return the sentiment. Scowl if you must, or make no expression at all. That would be safest.

(But you never do what's safe, do you?)

He produces a shot glass from his back pocket—"in case of emergencies," he tells you—and offers you a sip from the bottle.

The music drops out around you, and he fills the shot glass before you say yes or no.

"It's the best you'll ever have," he promises, and you feel yourself flush, as your lips curl into a grin.

Don't accept the drink. Don't accept anything from him. No good will come from it.

So you quaff the shot in one gulp, yes? Of course, you do. Foolish girl, always chasing wolves.

Fine. You took the drink, but don't take his number.

He won't offer it to you at first. He'll offer you nothing except that single drink. Anything more would breach propriety and propriety matters to him. You're a student and he's on faculty, teaching in some arcane department that never has enough funding. But that's not even the decorum that worries him most. His wife is here with him, a tiny thing flitting about like a lost pixie. Across the room, she laughs nervously and converses with acquaintances and flashes the occasional glance his way, though he hardly notices her. You want to tell him to go to her, but you like the way he keeps looking at you. Besides, you tell yourself, why should it bother you if it doesn't bother him? She's not your wife, your promise, your future.

Your fingers quivering, you pass his shot glass back to him, and he smiles again and drops his chin. His face—so ordinary a moment ago—sharpens with shadows and angles like a haunted forest at midnight. Like something that can't be trusted.

You excuse yourself and stand alone in the corner, but at the end of the night, when all the other guests have staggered home, he smiles one last time and, when he's sure his wife isn't looking, slips his phone number between your fingers.

You already know what you should do with it.

Crumple it in a ball and drop it at your feet.

Dip it in the last of the Bacardi 151 and set it on fire.

Stick it on your tongue and wait for the paper to melt into pulp.

Just don't save it in your phone.

There wasn't even space in your address book for that entry. And you already have two other William's in there, so how will you know one from the other?

When you get home an hour before dawn, a flush still burning your cheeks, delete the number. Erase it from your memory before your life falls out beneath you and you can't stop yourself from calling him.

But you don't need to call him. How old-fashioned of you to think the telephone is the only way couples court these days. The next day, he's already added you to Facebook and followed you on Twitter and Instagram. You follow back.

(You can't help yourself, can you?)

For a while, the two of you say almost nothing to each other. Just the usual "Great to meet you!" that appears so painfully ordinary from the outside.

And that's okay, because you have other problems to occupy you. Your dissertation is already four months overdue, and though she won't say it, your advisor loathes everything about you.

"You're a highly skilled student," she always demurs, "but sometimes that isn't enough."

What she means is there's no place for you. Not in your department and probably not in this world. So while you hate to admit it, this new man is a welcome diversion. A shameful one too, but thinking about him is still better than thinking about your empty refrigerator and emptier bank account.

(You wish you could eat course credits. If that were the case, you'd never go hungry.)

It starts quietly between you and him with Facebook likes and wink-and-nudge comments, a retweet here, an Instagram heart there. Infidelity blossoms in such small ways that it makes it easy to deny.

He's good at this, like maybe you're not the first girl he's picked out at a party. You're younger than him by more than a decade, but you still don't grasp these nuances of social media as well as he does, the way people converse and network and flirt without ever exchanging a true word between them. You do your best at it, but of course, your best isn't very good. Ask anyone. You're spectacular only at failing. You can't pick an apartment that doesn't include an army of cockroaches for roommates. You can't pick a car that doesn't throw a rod or catch fire or sputter out for no reason. You can't pick friends that don't abandon you at parties, and now apparently you can't pick a would-be lover who isn't married.

To assuage your guilt, you fancy this is all a game of make-believe.

You pretend at the party, you didn't see the glint of lust in his eyes.

You pretend you don't have his number like a filthy secret tucked away in your pocket.

You pretend it's all harmless until he messages you at three in the morning and your breath catches with the words you read.

Would you like to meet me tomorrow night? My wife is out of town.

Never accept an invitation from a wolf. That's a simple rule and one you should appreciate. All girls understand such a danger. But when a man isn't a wolf—not yet anyhow, the moon isn't right—and when the invitation is not a shrouded pathway into a forest but an entrée downtown with dinner and a Broadway play, how dangerous can it be?

(Would it be too on-the-nose if the tickets are for *Into the Woods*?)

You're in an Uber on your way to the theater when your mother calls. You don't answer. What would you say to her anyway? "I'm going on a date with a married man. How's your ladies group at church?" No, it's better to leave her to voicemail.

After the show, over red wine and a red tablecloth, he tells you everything you want to know about him. His eyes are greener than you remember.

When the restaurant shutters for the evening, he leads you to a waiting taxi. Since he lives on the other side of town—he's already told you his address three times—he doesn't join you. But as you climb in the backseat, he leans in and kisses your cheek and leaves a whisper in your ear before he turns and vanishes into the darkness.

The whole ride back to your apartment, his final words echo on repeat.

Come to me at home tomorrow night. I'll be alone.

A lie. If he gets what he wants, he won't be alone. That's the whole point.

In the morning, your mother calls again. This time, you answer.

"Where are you? Where are you going?" she asks.

Where are you going with your life? she means. She doesn't understand you and never has. You can't blame her.

After an hour of listening to her talk nonsense, you hang up with nothing resolved. This is how most of your conversations go these days. You try to talk to people—your friends, your family, hell, even strangers—and you try to listen, but everyone's words are a grab bag of gobbledygook, and nobody ever seems to answer you when you speak. They talk over you and under you and around you, but never *to* you.

This makes you certain you're extraneous, belonging nowhere at all.

But maybe that's not so bad. If you belong nowhere, you might as well go anywhere you please. So that evening, when the sun sets, you opt for his bed.

Anytime you feel lost, you imagine yourself in the same place. Wet earth squishes beneath your bare feet, and the wind whispers in your ear as you run—away from your apartment, from the city, from the life that never quite fit you the way you thought it would.

Into the forest. Into freedom.

When you were young, you were sure you'd one day become a witch with a gingerbread house, or a lady who soars over villages in a mortar and pestle. Instead, you can't even soar above your student loan debt; creditors, like the cockroaches in your pantry, always find you.

But tonight, you forget everything, as you crawl next to him in the dark. His skin smells of fallen autumn leaves and a home you've never known. Close your eyes and breathe him in, but whatever you do, don't memorize his scent. Remembering will only make this harder when it all ends.

And even a foolish girl like yourself knows it will end.

There are no trees and earth here like the ones in your dreams. This tangled forest is made of sweat and skin and satin sheets purchased at a bargain sale by a woman who should be here in your place, a woman who certainly trusts that her husband is alone in the bed they made together.

He leaves bitemarks on your flesh and you wrap your long legs tighter around him.

Afterward, he doesn't look the same. His features have elongated, his teeth sharpened. It was never a striking face. But now with your scent on him, he's something else entirely.

The morning after, you retreat to your apartment and make excuses into your coffee cup.

It was only one time.

His wife never has to know.

No one will get hurt.

Your hands tighten bone-white in your lap, and the pale swirls of cream in your mug neither judge nor absolve you. You tell yourself last night doesn't define you. One mistake doesn't define you.

But here's the truth: you were never a nice girl. When others your age were brushing their Barbies' long blond hair and playing board games like Mystery Date and Sweet Valley High, you were creeping out your bedroom window at midnight to dance in the center of toadstool circles. You knew the risks, a maiden alone among the shadows and capricious fair folk. That's why you did it.

Nothing is so fun as the forbidden. And now he's the verboten thing you desire.

You won't meet with him again. This is what a good girl would do.

But you already know it's not what you'll do.

The next week, his wife is back in town, but he still has plenty of free time. She can't watch him every moment of the day.

On a Tuesday afternoon, he invites you to a picnic in the forest.

"An escape," he says over the phone.

Although you only nod yes, never uttering a word, he laughs and says, "I'll pick you up in fifteen minutes."

He drives you out of town and leads you into the woods, and you smile like a fool all the way. In a moss-scented valley, he strips off your clothes, piece by piece, his hands steadier than they have any right to be. You relish his touch, but even more than that, you relish how he makes you forget. There is only this moment, and nothing beyond it.

When it's over, you lie back and play dead, your head lolling and eyes softly closed. You envision your body decaying in the sunlight as a band of wild animals crunch merrily on your bones. Part of you would rather die here now than go on living in a world where you don't belong. Though if you had a choice, you would simply stay here, alive and wild.

With the earth cool against your bare skin, you remember those solo dances at midnight when you were a girl.

"The devil's work," your mother said when she caught you, but even as she clutched the cross that hung limply around her neck, you knew she didn't believe that. If it were the devil's work, she would have grabbed both your wrists and dragged you to the nearest priest for exorcism. Holy water and holy verse, and you would have been good and right, the daughter she always wanted.

If it was the devil's work, that would have been easy. But it wasn't. It was your work. It was who you were and are and will always be. And try as she might, your mother could never cast you out of yourself.

The sun sets, and your lover snores next to you, the guttural noise almost a growl. You breathe in, and all around you, the earth whispers your name.

You tell yourself it's only a trick of the wind.

Here's a twist: instead of leaving your lover, let him leave you.

When you awaken, it's nearly dawn, and he's gone. You scramble for your clothes and call his name, but nobody, not even the wind, bothers to answer.

In a forest darker than heartbreak, a wolf will always abandon a girl. That is in his nature.

It is also in the girl's nature to find her way out again. These tales are familiar for a reason.

Close your eyes, and turn three times in a circle. Then look again, and take the first path you see. It might not be the right way, but it's better to choose a direction than to stand still and wait for the shadows to devour you.

But you don't have to worry. Your instincts in the forest are better than you think. Better, perhaps, than even a wolf's. The first path you pick is the correct one. If by correct, you mean the one that will lead you back to him. You find him waiting for you at the car.

"Where were you?" he asks, his voice as steady as the seasons. "I thought you were right behind me."

After he drops you off at your apartment, all sweet smiles and apologies, steel yourself against him. Don't answer his calls or his texts or his whiny Facebook messages. Most of all, never click like or love or retweet on his passive-aggressive posts about *someone* who won't listen to reason. (Try not to pity his wife when she adds comments like "What's wrong, baby?" or "tell me about it tonight" or simply "???")

He, of course, doesn't pity her. He pities himself. And you thought only silver bullets could take down a wolf. It turns out a harsh word or no words at all wound just the same. Such delicate little beasts, aren't they?

When you finally break down on a lonely Sunday evening and answer his call, expect his contrition, as worthless as it comes.

"I was telling the truth," he says. "The forest tricked me into walking away from you."

Don't believe a word he utters, but most of all, don't agree to meet him. Tell him instead you'll never meet him again. Especially not in his bed because his wife is out of town on another business trip. Especially not tonight. Especially not an hour from now.

Slip a compass in your pocket. You might not be venturing again into the forest, but this path is even darker, and you need all the help you can get.

He's waiting for you on his dim front porch. You go to him because you can't imagine another way.

He gazes at you like a stranger. Every time you meet him, he's a different version of himself, the green in his eyes brighter, his body gaunter or broader depending on the light. You think this is something he does on purpose, to keep you guessing, but tonight, as his skin tightens on his bones, you understand for the first time that he doesn't realize what he is.

A wolf. A monster. All the things you want and loathe and love and fear.

Upstairs in bed, you pull his body closer and whisper, "I hate you," and hope it's enough to chase him away.

Don't be surprised when it makes him desire you more.

You could still run. You know you won't, but you could.

On a Saturday morning in January, his wife finds your earring under the bed and guesses the rest. With the help of her sour-faced best friends, she moves out before sunset.

"We can be together now," he tells you, and you almost ask exactly what the two of you were doing up until this point if only now are you *together*.

But you shouldn't ask. You should just tell him no.

He pays for your broken lease and moves you into his bed. You, his lover, his mistress, the temptress with lips as red as... blood?

No, that's too obvious.

How about *lips as red as pomegranate seeds*?

That night, he prepares a welcome-home dinner for you, but don't take even one bite. Don't accept his invitation into the underworld, a domain that belongs to him alone. Again, every girl knows that.

(But of course, you swallow the seeds. Isn't that your birthright?)

Your first fight comes a week later, all broken glass and broken promises and broken you.

(If you had an iota of sense, it would also be the last fight.)

Soon, the scent of leaves on his skin is replaced with a wet-fur stench, and his teeth are so sharp you're afraid to kiss him. He isn't human anymore.

You wonder now if he ever was.

After the fight, he takes a sabbatical, and at his insistence, you drop out of school.

You're suddenly marooned in a life he's built for you.

Try to reach your mother for advice. She won't answer your calls.

It's indecent what you did to his wife, she texts.

Your mother's a good woman, a strong woman, a woman who does what's right. Not like the daughter she raised. A daughter who chases wolves, who's been caught by a wolf.

Try once—and only once, because you already know it'll be a waste of your time—to break up with him. Do it the old-fashioned way over a smudged booth in a late-night diner where the garish fluorescents turn your skin yellow and make him look more like a ghoul than ever.

"It's not working out," you say and the words taste so foolish on your lips that you nearly shriek at the absurdity of it all. You might as well have opted for *it's not you, it's me* or *let's stay friends.*

His body contorts in front of you. He's older now, and younger somehow too, like a scared child cowering in a corner. Your heart twists in your chest, but you harden yourself against it.

"It'll be better for both of us," you say.

But he shakes his head. "It's too late. We're tangled together. There's no separating us now."

You take a heavy gulp of your too-hot coffee and wish he wasn't right.

The next day, when you go out alone for groceries, don't head straight back afterward. Circle the neighborhood five or six times, and try to forget where you live. Try to forget the shape of the little blue Cape Cod that smears into all the other identical facades on the street. Try to forget his face. If you can get lost in the forest, maybe you can get lost here too.

Give up after an hour, and go home—to his home—because these days, he's the only thing you remember. Even if you wish you could forget.

Prepare a dinner of dry roast beef and boiled potatoes. Afterward, when he retires to his study to read by a fire that you never see him light, skulk upstairs to the bathroom. Lock the door. Shove your fingers down your throat, and heave up your insides. Maybe the pomegranate seeds lodged in your heart will come loose and you'll be able to escape.

Don't be disappointed if when you're done, it's only bile and undigested potato in the browned toilet water.

Go on a hunger strike. Cook nothing and eat nothing, and try not to exist at all.

(Gag when his clawed hands spoon stringy broth down your throat, as he begs you to stop hurting him.)

At the stroke of the witching hour, sneak out of bed, and while he sleeps, pack your bags, holding your breath as you tuck your dresses and cardigans and heirlooms like your grandmother's wedding ring inside your luggage and zip up what's left of your life.

The holding-your-breath part is essential. That's the only way the magic will work. And you'll need magic to have any chance at all.

You're in the doorway when you hear him stir behind you.

"Don't go."

You still don't breathe out. You can still escape.

"I need you."

He says it like you're life-giving, like you're air or water or the hot blood pulsing through his veins. You're none of these things. You're not even good for yourself, so how can he possibly expect you to be good for him?

You whirl around to face him. Once again, he looks different. His hair has turned to straw, weak and wilted around his ears.

"Please," he whispers, and the sorrow tinging his voice is enough to force the air from your lungs. In spite of yourself, you exhale, and with the fragile magic now shattered, you climb back into bed and cradle his quivering body in your arms.

Pretend you're someone else. This should be easy. You forget what life was like before you were here in this place. Before your heart became indentured to his.

Maybe if you pretend hard enough, he won't recognize you anymore.

(He does, of course. He says he'd recognize you anywhere. "In any shape," he claims.)

Try leaving in a storm.

Take nothing with you this time. Just slip out the door, and with gray clouds as your disguise, don't look back.

(But he'll follow you down any street and drag you home. You'd be almost disappointed if he didn't.)

Try fire.

Wait until after dinner when the pyre in the study ignites and use his own flames against him. He won't even be angry when you douse him with kerosene and toss a fiery dishrag at him. He must have expected this. You're so predictable.

And besides, it's all for nothing. His skin refuses to burn.

(What are monsters made of anyhow? Titanium and nightmares?)

Try water.

Invite him into a lavender-scent bath and make love to him like it's the last time.

(You hope it is.)

When his head drops back in ecstasy, press down on him with your body, and force him under the water. Watch him struggle. Watch him survive. His lungs overflow with liquid, but he never stops breathing.

(He's part of nature, after all, and nothing is so natural as water.)

Try earth.

Spike his Friday night cocktail with crushed sleeping pills and drag his dozing body to the nearest park, the one with the overgrown paths nobody uses. Inter him six feet deep, or dump him in a shallow grave. The choice is yours, though the outcome will be the same.

(He'll climb out of his makeshift tomb and back into bed before dawn. Next to you, beneath the white sheets, his cold body will smell of earthworms and betrayal and things that are rotten but still not dead, and you'll hate yourself a little when you pull him closer and inhale the scent. You like it more than you should.)

You resign yourself to the truth: your lover is more resilient than Rasputin. There is no exterminating him.

The only way out is to run. But you're not sure you can do that anymore.

You need help.

Call your mother again and convince her to meet you. She agrees, which inspires a flutter of hope in your chest, but it's only so she can criticize you over watercress sandwiches and Waldorf salads at a local bistro.

"Sometimes I've wondered how you could be mine," she says, the tines of her fork click-clacking against the pristine porcelain plate. "Sometimes I've pretended you don't belong to me. That you belong to those places where you used to run. Maybe you're more wild animal than human."

There's no malice in her voice when she says this, just a lifetime of quiet resignation.

You toss a wad of dollar bills on the table, the last of your stipend from college and enough to pay for both your lunches, before you trudge out of the restaurant without saying goodbye, your head down and heart heavier than before.

There is one last person to seek out, someone to whom you owe penance more than any other.

His wife.

Invite her to a coffeeshop, the closest to neutral ground you can get.

"He misses you," you lie across a table. "Please come back to him."

She tosses her head back and laughs before she sets her gaze on you. As though she's been practicing for a lifetime, she says one word.

"No."

Your chest tightens, and it occurs to you perhaps she was once a lonely girl at a party too.

She smiles before standing from the table. "Sorry, love," she says, "but he's your problem now."

It's only then you realize not every story belongs to you and there's always a chance someone else will get the happy ending you thought was yours.

In your heart, you wish her well.

And then you wish you were her.

When you return home from the coffeeshop, your body aching with regret, you lock yourself in the cellar and retreat to the dustiest corner. Alone in the dark, you force your calloused fingers into your mouth to muffle your screams. And scream you do, silently for hours until your throat is raw. You quietly hope he doesn't find you here, concealed within his own home.

Hiding is a half-hearted attempt, but face it: you're running out of escape routes.

In the dust and mildew, try one last time to remember.

Remember who you are and where you've come from and what you want.

Remember his touch in the forest, the way he stripped off your clothes, piece by piece. Without you realizing it, he stripped away your life too—your home, your routine, your future.

But maybe that isn't so bad. You never wanted those things, and now without them to shackle you, you can become what you've always been.

A monster hiding in plain sight.

"Take me back to the woods," you say and he smiles.

"I can't see you," he whispers in the dark, and you grin to yourself as you drop your pocket compass at his feet, and slip into the shadow of the tallest tree. This is where you belong, where you've always belonged.

You were never chasing wolves. You were chasing yourself.

The moon is right and your fingernails lengthen into claws, sharp enough you could rend his flesh with a single swipe.

But you don't touch him. There's more than one way to defeat a monster. In a veil of fog, you inch away until he's a mere inkblot in the distance. He's the lost one now. Lost in the forest. Lost without you. This is crueler than death and it makes your body sing.

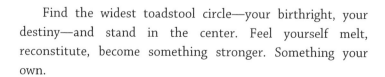

Find the widest toadstool circle—your birthright, your destiny—and stand in the center. Feel yourself melt, reconstitute, become something stronger. Something your own.

All around you, he screams your name. He'll scream for a long time, perhaps a day, perhaps a lifetime. His desperation might haunt you from every deadfall and valley, but you just laugh because he was wrong. He said he'd recognize you anywhere, in any shape. But you're finally yourself and standing right in front of him, and he cannot see you, cannot fathom you.

This is right. This is the only way you could have escaped, by becoming everything a proper lady should never be—feral and free.

Walk away now. Just smile and walk away.

The woods are waiting for you.

IT BREAKS MY HEART TO WATCH YOU ROT

SOMER CANON

Love doesn't provide happy endings. All things end in death and death is rarely happy. Even the immortals don't believe that love carries that kind of power and though they love, they have different values from the short shining lights of the mortals. Love, beautiful thing that it is, hurts in the end. Immortals who dared to love mortals knew this too well.

Every Saturday she went to him and every time he knew her less. She took him away from the place with its sterile, yet filthy smell, and took him for a ride in his car. A car that he loved. A car he could no longer drive.

"What a great car!" He would exclaim in delight.

"Sure it is," she would answer. "It's yours."

He would look around him in confusion, and then, like a screen being cleared off, he would smile, the knowledge of the car being his own already gone. The horror of forgetting something that was once so dear to him hurt her. He had spent years rebuilding the car, something he had bought as junk for cheap and had molded into sleek chromed art with his own hands. It had been one of his greatest treasures, a source of immense pride. Now, he sat in it with the fresh delight of a child on a carnival ride, long forgotten to him were the intimate hours spent with the machine.

She would take him to his old barbershop where old men younger than him would snip the hair around his ears, give him a close shave, and put a hot towel on his face. Once, he had done this every Saturday for himself, a ritual more sacred to him than anything to be found in a church. Which was fine with her. She wasn't much of a believer. Most immortals weren't.

She would drive him to the park, to their bench that overlooked the river, and they would settle into a silence together, something that only she knew to miss as once familiar. She would look at him out of her periphery. The overwhelming scent of Barbasol wafting off of him didn't mask his vitality rotting away. He would forget that she was there and gaze hard at every woman's ass that passed them, waggling his eyebrows to himself. She'd hide a smile.

Sometimes he would remember her for a moment, drape his arm over the back of the bench and she would lean onto him, as they had done when he was young.

"You're a pretty great gal." He would say softly, putting his lips on her hair.

"Sure I am," she would answer. "I'm yours."

And it was true, whether he remembered her or not. Though she had known many before him and would certainly know many after him, for now, for as long as he was living, she was his. Just as she had promised.

But it was hard. She remembered still so vividly what he had been. You could see whispers of that man in the spotted creature with bulbous yellow eyes sitting next to her. Aging is a vile process for the immortals to witness, but watching it happen to a loved one, when there is no salvation from it, was agonizing.

He couldn't eat at his favorite places anymore, his ability to digest complex foods had long since gone. So when she noticed his chin dropping down to his chest, knowing that fatigue was pulling him down into the warm pool of sleep, she helped him back into his car. He would smile in delight and tell her again what a great car she had. She would hide the tears gathering in her eyes.

Nurses would flank him when he went through the double doors into the foul smelling place of slow rotted death and she would watch him shuffle away from her without so much as a goodbye, their day already forgotten by him. She'd flash a polite, pained smile at the receptionist behind the large round desk and she would wrap her arms around herself, missing him already, and she would leave.

When she got the call that he had died, "peacefully" the voice on the phone promised, she felt empty, not free. Mortality hurt even those intimately unfamiliar with it. Her love for him endured, even though he did not. But what good did that do anyone? More enduring than the object of her love was the hole he left behind. There's no happiness in holes.

Love didn't provide the real happy ending. There was no such thing between two lovers such as them.

WHAT IS LOVE?

CALVIN DEMMER

I inhaled the copper smell. The thirst almost quenched. My victim lay with their neck slit open and I took another sip of blood. The man had stumbled into our territory, no doubt seeking food to feed his family.

Would his family miss him?

Did they love him?

He wasn't from my tribe.

I would never kill one of mine.

Did it matter?

Isn't a kill still a kill?

A tear formed. It ran down my cheek, leaving a cold trail in its wake. I wanted to hate myself for what I'd done. The guilt would eat at my core all night. But I didn't get up. Instead, I lowered my head and extended my tongue.

I lapped from the crimson pool upon his chest.

It tasted so good.

What is love? It was a strange thought as I soared high above the savanna. I pushed the question from the fore of my mind and flapped my expansive black-and-white wings, sending gales across the land. The cerulean skies the village had known were gone. I'd beaten the heavens purple and pink, while towering cumulonimbus clouds gathered with their dark gray bases. At the sound of the thunderclap, the people below knew it was too late.

The die cast.

Their fate dealt.

I targeted the wooden huts, raining bolts of lightning their way. Beautiful infernos erupted. I aimed for the wooden enclosures next, sending livestock running in a frenzied stampede. The villagers stared at me with mouths agape and eyes threatening to pop out. The pandemonium reached its crescendo. I ignored the cacophony of screams between the cracks of thunder, indifferent to the chaos I'd brought upon the village.

I followed commands.

Lerato's enemies were my enemies.

Destruction had become routine.

As my wings grew tired, the devastation below bored me. The cracks within my soul demanded more than papering over. The chief of the doomed village burst from his hut, pulling me from my thoughts. The proud man wore feathers tied around his head and animal-skin attire rode his abdomen and hips. He shook his fist at me.

I directed an unrelenting bolt his way.

The white electrostatic discharge cracked. The chief could do nothing as he burst into flames. He fell, burned to a crisp.

The ash and bone that remained of the man pierced my mind. I'd done it. The typical excuse that I was following orders didn't work.

This was my crime.

They had all been mine.

Lerato, whom I'd obeyed for many years, thought I'd lost my mind upon my return. I told her that I needed more, that there was something missing, and that I wanted to feel love. I wanted to exist as more than a tool of war and revenge.

Her jarring laughter crawled over my back like a group of millipede. She stopped, realizing I was serious. Her mood turned icy. There wasn't much she could do. Mother may have owned me, but Daughter's magic was nowhere near as powerful. The witch doctor threatened me, cursed me, and then warned me never to return.

I didn't intend to.

Changing to my human male form, I journeyed on foot toward urban civilization. The people of my village called me many names: the flying beast, bird of death, monster—

Most people, however, knew me as the impundulu, the lightning bird.

But long ago, I had a name.

Dingane.

Being an impundulu shrouded me in myth and legend, as different cultures believed different things. The power to transform was mine, from wing to hand, from beak to face, from bird to man. I created storms, used lightning, rain, and gales of wind to bring annihilation. Over the centuries, many of the witch doctors I'd served released this form of destruction upon their foes.

The impundulu are sanguivorous. I craved blood, like a screen vampire. Insatiable and revolting, I drank until full. My kind was rare. The last time I'd seen another like me had been over two centuries ago.

I inhaled deeply. It had been many years since I'd been around the impatient people, roaring vehicles, and the plethora of buildings in a city.

The first day city people came at me like a rogue bull elephant. By night, I'd gained some understanding of how things had progressed since my last visit. The rules of social etiquette fluttered back to mind.

Seated at the bar in a cocktail lounge, wearing a white button shirt and pair of dark denims I'd purchased from a thrift store, I found a groove and knocked back a few of the fiery drinks on offer.

It didn't take long to attract attention from a female of the species. After a wink and wave, a tall, slender woman with black dreadlocks approached me.

"You look like you've had a rough day."

"More than you know."

We traded chatter.

"Are you hungry? Have dinner with me. My treat," the woman said.

"Yes, that would be lovely," I said.

The gold I'd exchanged earlier had bought me less local currency than I'd expected. The price of things had gone up since the last time. I followed her to her table, looking forward to the free meal.

"Perks of recent divorce," the woman said once we sat. She took a sip from her glass of wine. "Freedom."

"That's nice."

"I have to warn you, though—I'm a bit of a cougar," she said, making her hand into a claw. She growled.

Could she shape-shift?

Was she intoxicated and talking nonsense?

I nodded, unsure of how to react. I'd seen the cougar species many years ago on a long voyage across a giant sea. The animal was not unlike Africa's lions, but this woman looked nothing like them.

After dinner, we shared a few drinks. The woman complimented my looks. I reciprocated. And like a simple spell cast, we retreated to her place. My intentions had been pure. I wanted companionship—a preview of love. The intimacy warmed within unlike anything had in ages.

I awoke in the small hours with a thirst for blood. I was a man lost in a desert, desperate for a glass of water.

She was there.

She was asleep.

Her pumping heart teased.

Her blood tasted sweet.

The second night came. I intended to behave. I met a brunette named Sasha at a smoky jazz joint. Her youthful face demanded attention, her body mesmerized, and her soft brown eyes promised much. After a few smooth whiskeys, I found myself at her place. The passion and intimacy fueled me like no battle had. I could get used to such feelings.

I managed to ignore the night's blood call.

In the morning, intimacy tugging upon my burdened soul, I told her my story.

"Oh, stop now. What kind of girl do you think I am?" Sasha chuckled. "If you want to role-play, just come out and say it."

"I'm serious. I can change into a bird, like that," I said, snapping my fingers.

"Let's see then."

"You won't be scared?"

Sasha shook her head.

I reached out my arms. Fear and excitement coursed through me. If I was to find love, I had to be open. There could be no secrets.

Could Sasha handle it? Apart from the witch doctors, I'd yet to find another who didn't flinch when I transformed.

"Okay," I said, "here goes."

I didn't change. A sound in the back of my mind stopped me. It was a voice, soft at first, but it grew louder as I focused. A woman chanted. Other sounds followed: the cha-cha-cha of a rattle and then the beat of a drum. Cold sweat formed on my brow.

The voice was Lerato.

What magic was this?

I took a step back. Dizziness shook me. My body swayed as if I were on a boat while rocky waves attacked. Sasha's lips moved, but I couldn't hear her over the chanting and other sounds. She waved her arms at me, concerned. I couldn't respond. Instead, I clenched my fists, fighting against the ominous tension within.

Its potency increased. Lerato chanted a curse and I was the target. She'd triggered an old, primal need deep within me. My attempts to fight it were forlorn.

My view blackened.

I awoke to a familiar aroma. The metallic smell invaded my senses and for a moment, ecstasy gripped me. I had to push the feeling away to find lucid thought. Blood covered the sheets beneath me. I turned my head. Sasha's lifeless body, also covered in the crimson substance, lay alongside me on the bed.

I sat up to inspect the damage I'd caused.

A slash ran a fissure across Sasha's neck. Eyes once filled with light, now looked up at me with emptiness. I'd lost the battle to my urge once again, killing a person who may have accepted me and may have even loved me. Agony reigned in my core and I lashed out trashing the apartment, smearing the walls and destroyed objects with scarlet handprints. The guilt swirled, but I slowed its cycles, remembering Lerato's chant. She'd exploited my greatest weakness and would never allow me to find love.

I cradled Sasha to my chest. Tears fell from my eyes. Lerato may not have had complete power over me, but I remained enslaved to her regardless.

I returned to my bird form and jumped out the window, sending shards of glass down to the world below. Into the sky, I soared.

There was only one destination for me.

Lerato stayed in a hut just outside the village. She invited me in. We ignored the uncomfortable vibe between us as we took seats around her table. There was no need to acknowledge what had happened with Sasha.

I wasn't sure what would come next.

"Would you eat with me?" Lerato asked.

I wasn't hungry and it was an unexpected request, but I accepted.

I waited until we were halfway through the meal before saying anything. My mind had already lined up the first question.

"Why did you do it?" I asked.

"Do what?" Lerato said. She licked sauce from one of her fingers.

"The girl, you made me kill her. You made me drink her blood. You made it impossible for me to fight my urge."

Lerato smiled. "It's unhealthy to go against your nature. I was trying to help you."

"That's a lie. You did it to punish me for leaving."

"You shouldn't have left. You're mine."

"I am not—" A sharp pain pierced my core. The world rocked on its axis, tilting.

I stood up, knocking my chair over. My chest contracted. Something was wrong, terribly wrong, and I was losing all my bearings. I took a step, hoping I headed toward the hut's exit.

The ground rushed toward me.

I opened my eyes to the night. Above me, the stars ruled the sky. I tried to move, but found myself stuck in a large black cauldron. Bubbles rose to the top of the water around me. The crackling of burning wood alerted me to the reality of the situation.

"You can't feel," Lerato said, stepping before me. "You can't move either. Breaking bread with those you've hurt is never wise. You should be more careful."

I couldn't speak. I could only stare at Lerato's hardened face. Her eyes narrowed on me. There was no mercy there.

"If I can no longer have you or control you, then I shall take what power I can from you." Lerato grinned. "I simply cannot have you going off again."

I smelled cooking flesh.

She leaned forward and whispered, "You're mine, forever."

It dawned on me that a little part of me would always live within her. No longer would I have to endure another new day's sun alone.

She had picked me.

I was her obsession.

Together we would wander the lands until Mother Earth called us home.

This was love.

HEIRLOOM
THERESA BRAUN

Rachel tilted back in her office chair, trying to shake last night's nightmare. The shock of her stomach being a round mountain of nine months had her patting her flat tummy when she woke. This was a common dream for women, merely symbolic of birthing anything new. The only thing new today was a patient, hardly warranting this kind of anxiety. And, she had been testing her motherly inclinations by volunteering to hold abandoned and premature newborns at the local hospital. Although it seemed she was making a difference, by lending her human touch, the experience confirmed she didn't possess a maternal instinct. The nightmare didn't make sense.

Rachel turned her attention to the mirror on the opposite wall, bequeathed by her mother who seemed to float in the reflection with an air of poise, pressing her opera glasses to the living room window like always, scouting for exotic birds with her bright green eyes as sharp as an eagle's. But the image evaporated like a hot shower's steam once Rachel touched the glass.

After the antique was delivered to her office the previous day, Rachel had to tip the maintenance man to secure the huge piece to the wall. The wood frame of the family heirloom was complexly hand-carved, the gold paint still bright in spots, but tarnished in others, dark grime deposited in the grooves. Edges of the glass near the frame were speckled with age. Its old character contrasted with the clean walls and Ikea furniture. But this was where Rachel spent most of her day, and it was where she wanted the reminder of her mother, the person who had encouraged her to study psychology.

Rachel's phone vibrated with a message from John. His full name popped up: *John Johnson.* His parents' lack of creativity still made her smile. He was free tonight, most likely eager to ask if she'd considered his marriage proposal. She sighed. He was too accommodating, too attentive, too understanding, and too open. It was smothering. When she had told him she couldn't have kids, he had graciously said that they'd adopt. Then, he had nervously twisted his mouth into the cutest contortion. She didn't have any interest in having children, no matter how adorable his lips were.

Hearing the outer door open, Rachel went to the waiting room, her heels clicking on the tile. This first appointment of the day was pro bono. The client had lost her job and insurance, but something about her story resonated with Rachel, who'd insisted that she keep coming for sessions.

"Good morning, Ashley. Come in."

Only in her twenties, Ashley dragged herself into the room in a wide-stepped waddle, reminiscent of a giant spouting *fee, fie, fo, fum.* Some days this amused Rachel. Today her thoughts cast a cloud of seriousness, something she shared with Ashley, who wore the expression of a pouting toddler.

"Bottle of water?" Rachel imagined Ashley as a kid, her now short choppy hair once long, bouncing with a child-like enthusiasm, and her khaki pants and striped T-shirt once a frilly dress.

Ashley clasped her hands in her lap after collapsing into the client chair. "I did it again." The red and black checkered rug stole her attention. "I'm pregnant."

Rachel gnawed the top of her pen. "I thought we talked about this." It was Ashley's third pregnancy since she'd been in therapy. Disappointed in her client's state, Rachel put her hand on her own stomach, details of the nightmare suddenly assaulting her thoughts. She had woken on a mattress in a primitive cave, the odor of earth and blood in the air. Rachel rubbed her forehead.

Ashley's gaze didn't leave the carpet. "I know."

"What happened?" Rachel refrained from inserting expletives, her disappointment in Ashley turning to anger, followed by a wave of empathy for the difficult decisions ahead. Rachel's dream fetus squirming and crushing her bladder was an uncomfortable blurring of the line between her and Ashley.

"The guy bought me a few drinks and the next thing I knew we were in the back of his van."

Exactly how many was a few drinks? They'd talked about waiting six dates before sex, the barest minimum being three dates. She watched Ashley spiral out, giving a play by play of the details. Peppered in between was commentary on what she should have done instead and how she was ashamed of herself.

Meanwhile, Rachel's mind kept running her nightmare's script. An old crone with striking emerald eyes had said this was Rachel's third baby—didn't she remember? *This one's destiny will be great.* A shaky hand had poured a half-shell of murky liquid into Rachel's mouth. An overwhelming fear for the unborn consumed her—a strong cord connecting her subconscious and conscious mind. It was all so vivid—she smelled the herbs and something putrid in the concoction.

"Have you decided what you're going to do?" Rachel asked during a pause, unable to will away her queasiness. Was this what morning sickness was like? It was possible Ashley was going through it already. But Rachel didn't know why she was so sick.

"I have to have it." Ashley balled her fist and put it to her mouth.

Why this one and why now were questions for another session. "Okay. So, it'll be more important than ever that we continue your inner work." Rachel pressed her lips together. "We don't have time for a regression today, but it will be a priority next time." Her forehead heated.

Ashley uncrossed her legs and doubled over, moping.

"So what's your plan for the next couple of days?" Swallowing a lump in her throat, Rachel eyed the garbage in case the contents of her stomach came up.

"Keep looking for a job." Ashley's hand cupped her stomach. "And stay out of bars."

"Good."

Ashley nodded and got up to leave.

As Ashley closed the door, Rachel thought about her own patterns. The passionate romantic love of equals was always out of reach. John's helping her up and down the stairs of her condo, and washing and folding her laundry while she recovered from her hysterectomy was sweet. But it made her weak, needy, and even worse, his kindness made him too feminine. So far no man had possessed the right dynamic, the right fit.

Rachel sipped the cold coffee on her desk to combat the emotional exhaustion. She had ten minutes until her next client, who, according to his file, had only been giving one-word answers during sessions. Fortunately, her petite frame and youthfulness, which made her look like a teenager from afar, had something to do with her ability to break tough cases.

That was the reason for the picture of the cat admiring a reflection of a lioness sitting on her desk, a gift from John, who also happened to be a therapist.

Rachel tapped into that energy, walking taller, as she went to the door.

The patient's arms and chest filled out his button down and his jeans were on the tighter side. Intense dark eyes were framed by neatly styled brown hair—a deliberate flair at the hairline, probably done with styling gel. Black rimmed glasses, magnifying his gaze, were perched on his face.

"Mr. Wilcox?" She extended her dainty hand and his swallowed it. "I'm Dr. Conrad." Something about him made her insides jumpy. Scads of clients had a criminal past, so it wasn't that. He triggered an incredibly disconcerting uneasiness impossible to explain.

Stepping further into her personal space, he smelled of cigarettes and maybe scotch.

She endured the uncomfortable closeness while he gave her the once over. He smirked. An apathetic recklessness lurked in his glare.

She kept a professional expression, which was rather like resting bitch face, and fiddled with her earring. "Would you like a water?" After motioning for him to help himself at the mini-fridge near her desk, she grabbed the manila folder and legal pad from the side table.

He took the water to the window, setting it on the sill. After pulling out an airplane-sized bottle of alcohol from his pocket, he proceeded to mix himself a cocktail.

Almost laughing aloud, Rachel confiscated his drink. "You're not doing this here." It was an effort to sustain her expression as she dropped the bottle into the trashcan. "Have a seat."

He shrugged, ran his hand through the side of his hair, and then sat. He leaned back in the chair, his legs spread eagle.

Rachel took her seat. As she glimpsed the antique mirror, the glass appeared to tremble. It wasn't the first time her mind had played tricks on her under duress, so she dismissed it.

She tapped the pencil on her lips. "By now, you know how this works." Earlier in her career, she would have started with something simple like whether or not he easily found her office, or maybe how long he had lived in Ft. Lauderdale. That only wasted the appointment. The goal was to expedite wellness. "What brings you in?"

He crossed his arms. "Got to be here, else I won't see my kids."

Rachel sat stiffly upright, hands folded. "Okay, so tell me more about that. Why is it mandated?"

His face relaxed and his eyes softened. Her directness disarmed him. "Maybe I have *mommy* issues."

Rachel's eyes widened. "It appears more serious from the documents I have here." She tapped the pad and folder in her lap.

"It's complicated." He twisted the old-looking silver ring on his pinky, his eyes narrowing.

The fact that he possessed the air of a mafia boss planning his next hit amused her. The way he kept playing with the ring made her think that either he had a form of OCD or it was an extension of his presented manliness.

The mirror jangled on the office wall, putting it off kilter.

"Did you see that?" She leapt up to prevent her family heirloom from crashing to the floor.

Her client might have continued speaking, but Rachel didn't hear it. The room was like a wind tunnel. She slowly put one foot in front of the other until she faced the mirror. Her reflection stood in a charcoal gray pantsuit, her straight chestnut-colored bob curled up at her sharp jaw. An unseen hand pulled her through the mirror. Her vision blurred—everything was funhouse trickery, colors and shapes morphing, until the world crisped and focused once again.

She stumbled onto the dirt, now in sandals, kicking up grit between her toes, and looked down to see her usually pale skin was bronze. Thick, wavy brown hair cascaded over her shoulders.

She blinked. Her bosom was more ample and her hands lacked the pink polish she always stared at while on the phone back in her office. Supple suede covered her body. Silver armbands coiled around each bicep.

Sweat pearled all over her.

The day was sunny. A market bustled to her right, and an open plain lay silent to her left. Thatched roof buildings dotted the horizon. A wicker basket dangled on her arm. A horse-drawn wagon heaped with fruits and vegetables hurtled past her, the gravel stirred by the hooves and wheels disappearing in the distance.

Only a few steps away, a burly man emerged through a dust cloud. He wore a dark and tattered robe. His skin was tan, or grimy, and so were the rest of his features, his eyes shadowed by his protruding brow.

Weathered hands with dirt-encrusted nails swiftly gripped her by the arms and forced her over his shoulder. She dropped the basket and screamed. He scurried to the covered wagon rolling closer and threw her inside. Her legs brushed something hard suspended at his waist.

Then everything was like scraps of memory from a drunken night out. A dry rag was stuffed in Rachel's mouth. Rope bound her wrists and ankles. As the binding tightened, scraping her, she moaned. There was more than one man in the wagon, but she didn't know how many. Their faces floated around her like levitating severed heads. One of them had a maniacal, toothless grin.

Closing her eyes, she thought of her office—wishing to be back there. But instead of the scent of the vanilla plug-in, a rank stench of body odor and booze hit her nose.

"I hope we got the right girl," one of the captors said in a husky, faraway voice.

His hands outlined the generous curves of a woman before lifting Rachel's chin. He nodded. "Blue eyes. It's the right one."

She shook her chin free, wondering if this was a psychotic slip. The wagon bumbled along as the wheels struggled over the crude road. She longed to see the landscape in order to memorize any landmarks in the slim chance it might be useful.

Someone pulled her off the wagon and onto solid ground. One of the men untied her ankles and another tugged her by the rope tied at her wrists.

Rachel struggled for air, noticing the altitude change. A blanket of clouds swelled in the sky and a wall of black rock disappeared up into the thick, puffy haze. The base of the mountain housed a row of rounded openings.

One of the assailants yanked her leash, forcing her into a cave, her sandaled feet leaving grooves in the dirt. The damp atmosphere hung thick. Goosebumps ran up and down Rachel's arms before she warmed from the torches mounted overhead. A rusty odor of earth and blood pervaded the pitch darkness. She flinched and her eyelid twitched when she realized it was the same smell from her nightmare.

At the back of the cave an iron linked chain coming from the wall glinted, appearing serpentine along the floor.

The hairs raised along Rachel's arms and neck. Her heart pumped wildly as she recalled something at her captor's waist. Disappearing into the rolls of his flesh was a scabbard. She knew what she had to do. These circumstances seemed vaguely familiar like a scene from a movie.

The jailer loosened the ropes at her wrists. And as if she'd done this before, everything unfolding in this very sequence, she jerked free and slid the ropes off. Grappling with the folds of the man's belly, she ripped the dagger from its sheath. It was oddly comfortable in her hand. Gripping it tight, she swiftly plunged the steel into his heart, leaning on the blade, driving it deep.

He fell in anguish. His eyes bulged in surprise as he groaned. The chain clinked to the ground and his knees buckled. Rachel pushed him onto his back, pinning him with her legs. She drew the dagger from his chest and stabbed him again and again. Blood sprayed her face and neck, dripping along her skin.

His hands fell limp at his sides and his eyes lost their life.

Coming out of a trance, not fully realizing what she'd done, she let the weapon thump to the ground. At the sound of a commotion at the cave's entrance, she picked up the dagger and slithered into the shadows.

"Find her!" one of the men cried.

She had a sense she had lost time. Someone clutched her wrist, squeezing it until the knife thudded in the dirt.

She tried to wriggle free, but hands were all over her. Fingernails gouged her skin as the men yanked her arms and legs into the air, carrying her. At the wall, the chains clinked as they secured her wrists and ankles. She slid in resignation to the floor, hanging her head.

"She's *not* like all the others," the captor said as he examined the corpse at his feet.

"Apparently it's not just them blue eyes." The other one snorted and wiped his nose with his filthy hand as he ogled Rachel. "She's a fighter. Wonder if she has any *other* talents." His laugh betrayed impure thoughts.

Rachel curled into the fetal position. The sound of the chain echoed and faded into the recesses of her mind. Everything got smaller and smaller until she closed her eyes.

When Rachel came back to awareness, she lay on a coarse and lumpy mattress.

Mottled in her head were bits of a dream. She was blonde, long flowing hair spilling from under a silver headband encrusted with red stones. A silver belt cinched a leather bodice and short skirt hanging in strips. She swung a leg over a man sitting in a crude throne-like chair, her thigh high boot brushing his hilted sword. Pulling the blade from its sheath, she set it down on the banquet table. He smiled in anticipation, eyes turning black as if possessed by a demon. She held onto his face, putting her lips to his, his excitement evident beneath her.

Why her subconscious chose some Xena Warrior Princess fantasy, Rachel had no idea. Her mind was like the endless reflection of two mirrors facing each other. She was in a dream, having another dream. It was extremely disorienting, especially since she had no way to tell how much time had elapsed. For a moment, she identified with someone with multiple personality disorder.

Where she lay now, the walls were animal skin instead of stone. Cast iron caldrons of light stood at the four corners of the tent's dim interior. The flames rhythmically blazed up and dipped.

The tent flap peeled open and a man in a black robe strode through it. Whether he came from outside or from some other dimension, Rachel wasn't sure. He poured himself ruby-colored wine into a cup from a dulled iron pitcher. A prominent silver ring on his pinky finger shimmered in the firelight as he cast his head back to drain the liquid. He wiped his lips with an "Ah-h-h" and fingered the ring.

Rachel's heartbeat sped and her body trembled. She clutched the woolen blanket covering her. Her naked body was sore, especially down below. Her abdomen seemed tired and loose, her breasts swollen and full. She guessed this was the sensation of a new mother. Could she really have been in this place for over nine months?

After running his hand through his dark hair, his eyes narrowed. A twinge of unnerving memory struck Rachel. She knew she had seen that gesture before, and those deep-set eyes hiding malice and mayhem. Here, his penetrating glare burned with ownership.

As this familiar man stepped with determination to Rachel, her every muscle tensed. He squatted beside her. Fighting the urge to look away, she surmised she didn't get this tent upgrade by being meek and malleable. Boldly, eye to eye, she gulped deep breaths.

He stroked her like a cat while she gently took his hand and studied the ring. A blood-colored stone sparkled. Filigrees and scrolls decorated the silver setting. What could have been ancient symbols were marked on either side, continuing to the underside. She rubbed it with her thumb, recalling Wilcox fiddling with his ring. This man exhibited the same obsessive connection with his object of power.

"I am very pleased," he said as he freed his hand. "You have delivered your promise."

"My promise?" Rachel asked.

"Yes, this time a son, a protégé." The corners of his mouth turned up slightly, like a gladiator who had just slaughtered his foe in the middle of an arena.

How could she have made such a promise? Then she remembered her pregnancy nightmare. *This one's destiny will be great.* Is that what the ancient woman had meant?

"In fact, I'm *more* than pleased." His eyes went demonic black as quickly as ink bleeds through cloth.

Rachel shivered and drew back.

He grabbed her at the shoulders and mounted her. The scratchy blanket slid from her breasts. She whimpered as the pressure of his body on hers turned her soreness to sharp pain. His hand ready to rip free the covering, Rachel fought the urge to shrink away.

"Please." She violently drew up the woolen barrier, pressing it close.

The back of his hand thwacked her across the mouth and she tasted coppery fluid on her tongue. "You forget I'm your *Master*," he said with a growl.

His eyes were so black. She got lost in the void where the guilt and shame of submitting festered. Her whole life had been a struggle to take her power back and now she had to give it away. "Yes, of course, M-master." The title stuck in her throat.

His inky eyes bored into hers, taking her deeper than before. She longed to look away, but didn't show weakness. So he stepped inside of her, making himself at home in her secret places, coaxing her shadow self to come out and play. Then he raised her invisible puppet strings and took hold of her will.

He flung his robe aside as he rose onto his knees. A musky scent of essential oil infiltrated the air. His gaze fell upon his readiness, and Rachel knew what he wanted. She sat up, took him in her mouth, and shut her eyes tight while he grunted in satisfaction.

When he finally tired and rolled over to sleep, Rachel got to her feet, wrapping the blanket around herself. The fires were dying in the caldrons, but a faint illumination remained.

She spun on her heels to survey the tent. In the far corner, propped against one of the beams was a gilded mirror, making the space seem double the size. She stepped closer. This was a newer version of the antique hanging in her office. The curves of the carvings were the same, yet the gold paint seemed fresher and there was less grit hiding in the grooves. No signs of tarnishing under the glass yet. For the briefest of moments, Rachel swore she saw the image of her mother, but when she examined the reflection, only the tent was behind her.

Putting her hand to the surface, it became liquid, like the rippling surface of a pool. When her body broke through the permeable barrier, she had no idea whether she was alive or dead, awake or dreaming. In this limbo, she transformed. Looking down, her skin lightened and her body slimmed. The water-like portal pulled her through and back into her office.

Standing on the area rug, she turned to the antique mirror behind her.

She patted her belly, grabbed at her breasts, and dug her nails into her wrist.

Her face in the reflection went white. She was in her red Calvin Klein dress and a black blazer, but didn't recall the last time she wore it. Her legs went rubbery.

At her desk, she lifted papers in search of her phone. Her hands trembled.

A knock sounded on the office door. "Doc, ya in there?"

She knew that voice.

Standing paralyzed, she considered ducking under the desk in case her door was unlocked. With her luck, he'd find her cowering under the furniture. That was a sure way to have to terminate the therapy and to ruin her reputation.

Whenever a performer gets just enough mojo to go on stage, even if deathly ill, that's what Rachel mustered. A little winded, she opened the door. "Mr. Wilcox. Come in."

"Call me Rick, will ya?" His voice rang forth cheerily, the smell of alcohol on his breath.

"We'll keep it Mr. Wilcox." All of her other clients were on a first name basis with her, a sign she was comfortable with *them*. She went to her seat, the pad of paper and folder already on the side table.

Her patient sat and palmed the side of his hair. He inhaled deeply, clenching his jaw and twisting his ring.

She swallowed, fighting off the memory of his dick in her mouth. The burn of guilt and regret filled her. It was the ultimate client-therapist violation.

"So tell me—m-more—about your childhood." The pencil shook in her hand, so she rested it in her lap.

"I was short, scrawny, wore glasses." His finger pushed the bridge of his frames. "Was bullied."

It was the classic victim turned bully scenario, if he spoke the truth.

"But I told you all of this *last week*. Don't you have your notes?" He pulled his sleeves down and crossed his arms.

Her heart galloped. She scrutinized the pad and flipped a few pages. Sure enough, the details were there. "I—I see. How did that make you feel?" Her body quivered.

"I didn't. Got into some drugs, *remember*?"

Rachel jotted this down, not sure what was noted and what wasn't. "So you self-medicated. That's fairly normal." She was befuddled, unprepared. Like she was under the influence herself. "Do those memories still surface?"

Darkness bled into his eyes. "I want to talk about how I feel *now*."

"Yes." Her stomach contracted. Rachel clamped her notepad and the sweat dampened the yellow paper. "Okay, let's discuss what's on your mind."

"I'm overwhelmed by my thoughts. I'm not sure I can really say it out loud." His tone was laced with taunting.

"If you want to get *better*, we need to talk about it. It can't be that bad." But it could be *really* bad. And she couldn't detach herself from whatever was coming.

"I'm not sure I can."

Rachel squeezed the pencil. "How about this. You can write it down. I don't need to know. I can still help you." At the shelf, she obtained a blank composition notebook that was there for her clients to use as a journal.

Wilcox reached for the notebook. He licked his lips. Keeping steady eye contact with Rachel, he got up to help himself to a pen in the canister on her desk. Once returned to his chair, he began scribbling.

Periodically, his glare raked over her. She examined her calendar, searching for any stray notes or cancellations. Nothing amiss, appointments seemed status quo. She longed to scroll through her text messages and missed calls, but refrained. She had to keep a modicum of professionalism. Finally, the digital clock on her phone signaled the end of the hour.

After a subtle sigh of relief, Rachel said, "Well, our time is up. If you want to keep writing, you can take that with you." She folded her hands and squashed them together. Her fingers cracked.

"Why don't *you* keep it?" He got up and handed the book to her.

She followed him to the door and slid the notebook onto the shelf. "It will be here for your next visit."

He nodded. "Sounds good, doc."

And he was gone.

Rachel locked the door. Typically, reading through a patient's thoughts wasn't so pressing. She plucked the composition book off the shelf and flipped it open.

I just wanna get off the grid and shoot up heroin or oxycodone under the 42nd Street bridge. Hustling for cash on the corner. Shit, such freedom.

I'd hook up with my fav shorty. She thinks she's so in charge, wearing them suits. Hmmm... those get me hot. When she's sitting just a few feet away, I just wanna throw her down and rip her buttons off. I'd finally get a whiff of her panties. Mmmm...

She'd try her mumbo jumbo bullshit to stop me—but I'd make her do things she ain't done before. Things she ain't never do. Jesus, I can taste it—so sweet. I'd make her beg for it. Beg for me.

Can't you feel my hands, my cock inside you, Rachel? I've been dying to stick it to you since we first met. I know you want it. It's all over your face.

I can't wait till next time.

Yours forever, Rick.

Rachel smashed the book closed and tottered to her chaise lounge. The fact was that they *had* been intimate—how many times, during how many past lives or dimensions, she didn't know. It couldn't have been just the once. What about that Xena dream?

She wished she had liquor stashed somewhere in the office, but it was probably better she didn't. A possible DUI lined up perfectly with the guilt and shame-ridden energy she was currently emitting, so it was fortunate this wasn't the case.

Her hands quaked, still holding the notebook. Wilcox's mere presence threatened her on so many levels. It frightened her that his words didn't entirely repulse her. Was she attracted to him? Did she want him? She pushed that from her mind.

She'd have to report his inappropriate inclinations, especially since he was so good at turning the tables. He expected her to invade his privacy, to want to dig deeper into his psyche, his soul. Pretending she didn't read the notebook was going to be a big test.

Just then, the mirror winked at her with a flash of light. The antique witnessed all of her fears, insecurities, and her anger at being so vulnerable. It was somehow alive with her emotions, seeming to know her better than she knew herself, magnifying the sensation of powerlessness to unbearable levels. Since she couldn't destroy *herself*, she had to get rid of *it*.

Rachel jerked the golden frame forward and lifted. The wire on the back wasn't unhooking, so she tugged upward until it snapped and the mirror plummeted into her hands.

She lugged the antique, her arms extended as wide as they could go. Angling and navigating the doorways and stairwell, Rachel staggered onto the pavement.

She rounded the corner to the dumpster, heaped with bulging garbage bags. A sour smell blended with that of dead animals. Pizza covered in mold spilled from boxes. Chinese takeout containers leaked spoiled noodles. Padding burst from the ripped cushions of a chair. Rachel set the mirror on the concrete and wiped her temples. Then she picked it back up, hurling it with all her might onto the pile of refuse. It landed as if on a safety net, bouncing up and settling down.

The last thing Rachel wanted was for some other sucker to find this seemingly valuable treasure. So she scavenged through the neighboring vacant lot until she found a rock that she hurled at the mirror in the dumpster, cracking the glass and sending shards to pierce the trash bags.

After dusting off her hands, Rachel climbed the stairs. Once inside her office, she gasped at the mirror back on the wall, which glowered at her like a defiant child.

She hauled ass into the hallway, practically tumbling down the stairs. Busting through the rear door, she rounded the bend to the dumpster. Its open mouth was still crammed full of trash, minus the mirror.

Rachel heard a thwacking and recoiled. Thankfully, it was just one of the awnings on the neighboring building flapping in the wind. She inhaled a lungful of fresh air.

The idea of Wilcox creeping around in the parking lot, in the bushes, around every corner of the building, leaked into her mind. Hearing a rustling in the shrubbery behind her, she jumped. Hand over her heart, she turned to observe a stray tabby cat scampering through the leaves and scurrying away.

The question of whether or not the mirror lay somewhere in the mountain of waste still pressed upon her. She stepped to the rim of dumpster and reached for a two-by-four, using it to poke through the filthy contents. The antique was definitely not there.

Rachel kicked the side of the Dumpster.

Someone gripped her shoulder and she hopped. Her veins pulsed with adrenaline as she turned her head. To her relief, John stood there.

"Hey, I didn't mean to scare you. I saw your car and figured you had to be somewhere," he said, putting his hand effeminately to the front of his plaid button-down.

"Well, you scared me." Rachel's blood settled. "Congratulations."

"What are you doing out here with this junk? And why haven't you returned my calls?" John palmed the back of his neck, something he did when he was uncomfortable. "You look like you're wigging out."

"So sorry. I have a lot going on."

"Lemme buy you a drink."

"I need *more* than a drink."

"What's up?" His face looked worried, like he imagined this had something to do with *him*.

"This damn client Wilcox." Rachel noted John's insecurity and knew she wasn't making it any better. "He's got the hots for me."

"Why not? Good old Stockholm syndrome—plus, look at you." He raised a hesitant eyebrow. "What's the big deal?" His voice betrayed that it *was* a big deal.

Rachel had bigger things to worry about than John's jealousy and whatever other issues plagued him. "Things are getting weird."

"It's not the first nor the last time this'll happen. Confront it during your session. That usually works." There was a mixture of wounded puppy and a mustering of bad ass in his gaze.

"*Usually*, huh?" Rachel rolled her eyes. "Look, I need to finish some paperwork. Then I'm going home to crash." This standard therapist line was always the perfect excuse. He knew the plight firsthand.

"I thought we had plans. We still haven't talked." The hint of bad ass vanished.

"I'm so sorry. I can't."

"Look, I deserve some answers."

Rachel was impressed he was self-advocating. "I know. Just give me a little more time." Leaning in, she kissed him softly, hoping to appease him.

Her lips seemed to be a serum that gave him hope and patience. Nodding, a trace of a pout turning to a pucker, he fished his car keys from his pocket. It appeared he wanted to say more, to have the last word, but he grimaced and walked away.

Rachel entered the building, ascending the steps in slow motion. Pity and sadness were not the sensations she desired to experience with a romantic partner. Not that she wanted to be a rescued princess, either. That actually disgusted her. Where was the mate she could go head to head with? But other things cried out for Rachel's attention. When she opened the door at the top of the stairs, she half-expected to see Wilcox on the other side.

Thankfully, the hall was empty.

Back in her office, Rachel grabbed her purse from the desk. At the wall, she grasped the frame of the mirror with authority, heaving it from its place. She dragged the heirloom down to the backseat of her Toyota, planning to give the thing the same respect a serial killer gives his victim by leaving her abused and naked on the side of the road.

The next couple of days were like existing underwater. Rachel's thoughts were murky. She didn't want to move, much less to go in to work.

Once she left her condo, every strange man's face was Wilcox's. Had he been following her, she had no way of knowing. And babies were suddenly everywhere. One good thing she focused on: the mirror stayed gone.

Driving to the office, she couldn't shrug the recent dreams. Sometimes she'd be giving birth, the agony so unbearable she'd awaken. Then there were the times that Master was sweating on top of her while she underwent the sharp pinch of conception, like her body rejected their union and the point of creation. She often cried uncontrollably upon waking, unable to erase the residual cellular memory.

Her phone rang.

"Hello?" Rachel said.

"Dr. Conrad, it's Ashley. I'm sorry, but I'm not going to make today."

"Oh? Everything all right?"

"I'm not well. I missed some of my anxiety meds." Her voice was unsteady. "On my way to pick up a refill now."

"Are you sure you don't want to come in?"

"Thanks, but I just want to stay home."

"You can tell me about it now if you want." Rachel hoped Ashley didn't hang up.

"It's nothing. It'll go away with the pills."

Rachel sensed it wasn't nothing, but knew it wasn't time to push. "Okay, call me if you want to come in earlier. And don't forget to tell the pharmacist about your condition." Meds and an unborn child were not the recipe for health. But Ashley had to get ahold of her mental faculties, as that was equally important for the fetus.

"Thanks. Sorry about today." Ashley hung up.

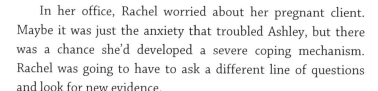

In her office, Rachel worried about her pregnant client. Maybe it was just the anxiety that troubled Ashley, but there was a chance she'd developed a severe coping mechanism. Rachel was going to have to ask a different line of questions and look for new evidence.

The outer door creaked. Rachel's palms moistened as she swung the office door open. "Come in, Mr. Wilcox."

He entered, carrying her mother's mirror. "Where'd ya want this?" he asked, propping the antique against his side.

Rachel blinked in rapid succession. "Where'd you get that?"

"In the hall. It's yours, isn't it?" He carried the mirror to the vacant wall where he looked up at the screw hole. "I'd put it up for you, but seems I'd need to bring some *tools*." Something about the way he spoke made the remark an innuendo.

Rachel cringed at his sleaziness, trying to forget his naked body pressing up to hers. It was so fresh and real, like he'd bedded her last night. "Just put it there."

He set it down. "Whatever you say." Then he took his chair, spinning his ring, a twinkle of red coming from his pinky.

After fetching the notebook from the shelf, Rachel sank into her seat. She tried to get a closer look at his ring, but he kept touching it. Firmly holding his gaze, she sat taller.

Wilcox eased back in his chair, his legs splayed. Uncapping the water she'd placed on the side table, his eyes softened and he appeared to repress a smile. "What'd ya want to talk about today, doc?"

"I thought I'd leave that to you." She pressed her lips together, immediately regretting giving him control over the conversation.

He ran his hand through the side of his hair.

That always sent a chill through her. She clasped her hands and gripped them tight. Her palms continued to dampen. "How about—?"

Wilcox crossed his arms. "How 'bout whether or not ya read that." He eyed the book.

Rachel's insides were like soda and Pop Rocks fizzing. Perspiration dotted her upper lip. "Did you *want* me to?"

He grinned. "I'm interested in what *you* want."

"None of this is about *me*. You're here to work out *your* issues. Don't you want to see your kids?"

"I want lots of things."

She wasn't going to fall into that line of questioning. "We all want things. I think we need to get to the source of what makes you tick. Tell me about your mother." It was probably too early to press, but she wanted to push back on him, and hard.

"My mother?" His eyes shifted. "I didn't have a mother."

"Did she leave? Did she die? Where was she?" Rachel bent forward and intensely peered into his eyes.

"I dunno."

Her instinct told her he was lying. "What did your father tell you?"

"I went from foster home to foster home. There's nothing to tell."

"That's not in your file."

"Not everything's in the file, doc." He pulled at the hair at the nape of his neck.

"You're going to have to tell me about your past if any of this is going to work." Rachel resisted the urge to swing her crossed leg.

"That's not happening."

"How about you write about it?"

His eyebrow raised in a dramatic arch. "So ya can read it?"

"I'm not going to read it. If you want, you can take the notebook with you." Rachel got up and snatched a pencil from her desk, handing it and the book to him.

Needing the buffer between them, Rachel moved to her desk chair. Her fingers drummed on her thigh as she pretended to go through her notes.

While the clock ran out, Wilcox wrote quietly, radiating impure thoughts.

She refused to look at him directly, until the buzzer sounded.

Wilcox tried to pass her the book, but Rachel refused to take it. He wryly grinned.

"You keep it this time, remember? Until you trust me, you're in charge of it."

"All righty." He pursed his lips.

"Just make sure you bring it next time." She regretted not addressing his fixation on her. Avoidance. If only she could avoid her entire life, including her dreams.

He stepped nearer, bringing a whiff of cigarettes. "No hug goodbye?"

"No, Mr. Wilcox." Her attention on the door, she willed him to walk through it.

"You're no fun." He thumbed one of his pockets.

"If you keep this up, we'll need to terminate therapy." In her peripheral vision, he adjusted himself at his fly. It took all she had to keep her line of vision aboveboard.

"See ya, doc." He put a finger to his lips.

"G-goodbye, Mr. Wilcox."

A startling thwack of thunder boomed, followed by that of a downpour of rain. Rushing wind howled. Rachel glanced at the window. It was still light outside, the sun peeking through the wispy clouds. But ominous ones floated in the mirror.

Not noticing the sudden storm brewing, Wilcox went for the door. He turned to regard her one last time with an air of knowing the secrets they shared.

Rachel drilled her gaze into him, wondering how privy he was to their past together.

A strobe of lightning flashed from within the glass, wiping her thoughts away. She plodded to the mirror, watching sheets of rain falling in the reflection. A spray of water sprinkled her face. Her feet stuck to the floor, even though she had the urge to run.

Wilcox reached for the doorknob to leave.

Wind swirled around her, pushing her closer to the antique until she leapt through the liquid-like surface. She changed physically, filling out with womanly curves. Her short hair spilled into thick, curly waves. Her skin darkened to soft mocha.

Rachel stood amid the cauldrons as the flames vaulted, generating long spectral shadows. Wind whistled outside and the pelting rain transitioned to the occasional drip on the hide of the tent.

A baby shrieked in the distance. Her heart hungered for the child not nursing at her milk-filled breast. She had never known such a painful separateness. It was worse than losing her mother. Worse than not knowing where her father was.

Following a cinching of the woolen blanket around her, she poured red wine into a pewter cup, slugging the liquid courage.

Rachel pushed the flap of the tent open—nothing there, except darkness and the smell of rain. Bare feet touched the muddy earth. Gradually her vision sharpened. There was a smoldering campfire on the horizon, human silhouettes gathered around it. They piled kindling, fanning the embers back to life.

Rubbing the chill from her arms, Rachel walked toward the cluster of people. A droning vibration traveled on the breeze. The closer she got, the more it sounded like singing. She strained to listen for the fussing of a child. Was the crying she had heard only her imagination?

Rachel squinted into the night. Smoke spiraled into the air and she whiffed frankincense and some unrecognizable herbs. An owl cooed nearby. She plastered herself against a massive rock.

Everyone in the crowd wore dark robes, fading into one another. Someone with long white hair spun around. Rachel locked with those maternal green eyes from her dream. The crone waved to the Master as Rachel contemplated her offspring's supposed *great destiny*. Would she ever know what that meant?

Rachel quickly slipped to the other side of the rock. Her fight or flight instinct prompted her to flee—but to where? Into one of the caves? Into the wilderness?

Just as she was about to run back to the tent, someone caught her by the arm. "I see you've changed your mind." His voice was calm, soothing.

Rachel peered into his familiar eyes, her knees buckling. "About what?"

He grinned, the pale moonlight highlighting his smooth face and the piece of upturned hair peeping from the hood of his cloak. "The tide of your soul is turning after all."

Rachel clutched the blanket tucked at her cleavage.

"You were *meant* to be here. Come." He motioned for her to follow. His congregation whispered amongst themselves, patiently waiting for a continuation of the ceremony.

"The gods smile upon us tonight." The low timber of his voice bellowed. The Master regarded Rachel with admiration and raised her hand into the air. After releasing his hold and she retreated, he signaled to his helpers.

Two hulking figures took their places at his side.

Rachel's legs wobbled and she closed her eyes. A sinister vibration enveloped her.

An infant wailed, shaking her back to awareness.

The Master took the bare baby and lifted it above his head. It squealed even louder.

The gathering sang words Rachel didn't understand.

"We offer this innocent life for your glory!" the Master proclaimed. Then he lowered the squirming newborn on the stone slab and waved his hands up.

The two other men closed in on the child. One man seized its arms, the other man snatched up the legs.

Rachel couldn't look away.

The baby yelled for loving arms.

Rachel fought the urge to run to the child—one that might have been hers. Her heart broke thinking of the life never to be. Emptiness and grief consumed her.

She shut her gaze, not able to watch after all. The chanting masked any horrific sounds. But Rachel's imagination saw the animation in the blue eyes go out like waning flames surrendering to the darkness. She put her hands on her belly, a tear sliding down her cheek. Her stomach turned.

The crowd's droning rose up and then died.

Rachel finally opened her eyes. A red spattering covered each murderer, their black eyes vacant. No blade in sight, they had used their bare hands.

The Master's bloody palms painted his face crimson. He loosened the top of his robe to draw a symbol with two fingers on his chest. He shoved what looked like raw flesh into his mouth before putting his hands together in prayer and bowing to the altar.

Everything went dark as Rachel's legs finally gave way.

She lay in the Master's arms, his lips touching her forehead. He lightly snored while cradling her body in what seemed like a loving embrace, spiked with a sinister power.

Her awareness was foggy.

The memories of the horrors around the campfire blipped through her mind like a television shorting out. She pried herself from him and climbed off the bed.

The mirror loomed in the same place, this time covered with a black cloth. Time seemed to carry on without her on the other side. It must have been the same here.

Rachel went to unveil the antique, the material pooling on the ground. Her hand touched the surface. In the reflection, a dark shadow rose from the man on the mattress. Its ghastly shape swarmed to her and hovered above her head. Eyes like black marbles burned hot red for an instant. A wicked sneer faded as the figure disappeared through the mirror, taking hold of Rachel's hand. It towed her through and everything whirled like a spinning kaleidoscope.

She sailed onto the carpet in her office, nearly floundering to the floor. The shadow rose up in front of her like a genie coming out of a bottle, before it evaporated.

Rachel scratched her head.

Someone knocked.

"One moment," she said, taking a look at her desk calendar. Then she realized she had no idea what day it was. Her hands covered her mouth. There wasn't time for her brain to process anything.

She took a swig from a half-consumed water bottle, hoping to ground herself.

After opening the door to the waiting room, Rachel sighed in relief. "Come in, Ashley."

The client sat, her back a bit straighter than the last session Rachel remembered.

Instead of noting the body language and commenting, Rachel searched the air, wondering where the shadow went— or what the hell could possibly happen next.

Rachel forced herself back into therapist mode, which was second nature. "Did the
medication help you?"

"Yeah. The next day I was better." Ashley picked at her fingernails. "It's a lot less,
but it still happens."

"What happens?" Rachel had to wrangle her attention. The blood. The innocent sacrifice. She repressed tears.

"I'll be like looking in a store window and there's a reflection—of something that's not
there."

Rachel perked up and her eyes widened. "These could be important projections of your mind. What do you see?"

"There's no sense to it. Sometimes it looks like a pile of baby dolls. Other times—"

"Can you describe the dolls?" Rachel scratched her nose, her lip quivering behind her
hand.

"They're naked. Some don't have eyes. Arms and legs are torn off. They're all scraped
up." Ashley's eyes watered.

Rachel shuddered. "How does this make you feel?" The source of Ashley's vision could be her abandoned inner child, the abortions she had as a young woman, or a sign she didn't want to bring a child into the world. But it was the coincidence of what Rachel just experienced on the other side of the mirror that tormented her. Her heart broke again as she mentally relived the slaughter.

"I'm so sad."

"It's okay. Allow yourself to feel. It's actually a strength. Honor it." But all Rachel wanted to do was make her own emotions stop.

Ashley wiped her eyes. "It doesn't feel like that."

Rachel's words sprang forth as if not her own. "Because you've been told not to feel, that your feelings didn't matter. But they *do*. They *do* matter. *You* matter. You're starting to realize that." If there was ever a time to face her own advice, it was now. She mattered. Emotions were power. However, it rang as psychobabble bullshit.

Ashley plucked a tissue from the box on the table and blew her nose.

There was more time in the session to kill before Rachel could wallow in her own problems. "Let's see if we can heal your inner child some more. We'll do another regression."

Ashley got up and reclined on the chaise.

Rachel led the client through some deep breaths and a descent down a spiral staircase. Meanwhile, there was a rewind of the Master telling Rachel he was pleased, that destiny brought her there. She literally stood by while it all happened. Her complicity was inescapable.

Rachel tapped her pencil on her chin to keep her present. "Once you get to the landing, what do you see?"

"It's dark. I don't see anything." Ashley's eyelids scrunched.

"It's okay. Just relax." She swung her leg back and forth.

Several seconds passed. Ashley's head rolled from side to side. "It's dark."

"Good. What else can you tell me?"

"I hear babies crying. So many babies. I can't see them, but I know they're there."

Rachel held her breath. "Trust what you're sensing. Do you see anyone? Do you see your inner child?" She bit her nail until she bled.

"There's a man. He's tall. I only see a shadow."

"That's okay. Does he seem familiar?" Uncrossing her leg, Rachel hunched forward.

"He tells me he's my father. But I'm scared."

Confronting father figures was always a good thing in therapy, but a strong apprehension paralyzed Rachel. "Is he someone you've known in this life?"

"No." Ashley's head lolled. "There is something wrong with his   eyes."

Rachel jumped in her chair. "What do they look like?"

"They're black. They look like holes."

"He can't hurt you. I'm here." She bit her lip, attempting to believe the lie.

"Yes, you're my mom. You want me away from him."

"I'm *there* with you?"

"Yes."

"What do I look like?"

"Tan skin. Eyes so blue. Like they're now."

Rachel forced an inhale. "Do you know what you're doing in this place?"

"No. You won't tell me. You're crying and saying to forget, to leave and never come back."

"Where is this place?"

Ashley paused, her head shaking. "I don't know. Carpathian something. Somewhere in the mountains. A long time ago."

The connection between their experiences became concrete as Rachel relived snippets of her cave abduction. The lines of subject and therapist blurred again. "Are you getting anything else?"

"No. You push me back to the stairs, telling me to leave."

"Why?"

"Because it's dangerous. The present can be altered." Ashley's forehead crinkled.

That was the point, to heal past and present, creating profound change. Rachel had done regressions many times. It wasn't dangerous at all. "That's okay. You are there to *release* the past."

"You're saying something about the mirror."

Rachel gripped her pencil tight. "Oh?"

"Something about not going through it?" Ashley thrashed her head back and forth, her body stiffening.

Nothing made sense, yet it all made sense. Was it a past life? Was it their alternate selves? Rachel had read that we all have counterparts existing in other realms at the same time. "Okay, it's time to climb the staircase. With every step you are more and more relaxed..."

After Ashley had gone, Rachel stood by the window, watching the clouds wander, hoping to calm down. They morphed, creating fluid shapes. A profile of a man with a beard became a stork. Then like an apocalyptic nightmare, she swore the entire sky washed with crimson. Blood. Motherhood. Birth. Life. Death.

Strangely, the portal hadn't been active today. As much as that was a relief, Rachel contemplated what was different. There had to be some catalyst that activated the phenomenon.

Glancing down at the courtyard, she noticed someone sitting on the bench. His legs spread apart and his arm stretched out along the top. That signature curl of the man's hair was just like Wilcox's. He peered up at her window. His dark eyes flashed in the sunlight while he puckered his lips, kissing the air.

Rachel's heart hammered. She wanted to duck out of view. Instead, she stared right at him. A blue jay landed on a nearby branch. When she turned her attention back to the bench, Wilcox had vanished. How she didn't detect his departure, she hadn't a clue. Was he even there at all?

She went to examine the mirror's age spots to clear her thoughts. The flecks of brown-gray splotches dotting the edges looked like eyes, and she wondered what they'd seen coming and going. Did her mother ever have any experiences like these?

Putting her hand flush against the surface, she studied the duplicate hand outlining hers. The surface didn't ripple. Nothing amiss caught her eye in the reflection. The horrific game being played with her soul, with her life, on the heirloom's terms, infuriated her. She longed to blame it all on Wilcox, but he wasn't pushing her through the portal.

And then there were the dreams. The memory of the latest one shot into her mind. Her gut wrenched with starvation as she stared at a bowl of raw meat. The cold glob of flesh was wet with blood. It dripped through her fingers when she slurped the last bits into her mouth. In the mirror's reflection, runnels of red dribbled from her lips and gore covered her teeth, the shrill cry of an infant ringing in her brain.

Standing in her office, sorrow made her want to shriek and drop to the floor. She had to find a way to end it all. Rachel grabbed her purse from the drawer and pocketed her phone, glimpsing the mirror glimmering at her in the late afternoon light. Passing out on the couch was the only way to forget.

When outer door squeaked, she braced herself for it to be Wilcox. Digging her hand in her purse, she gripped the gun she had started carrying, her finger searching for the trigger.

Rachel let out her breath and loosened her hold on the gun as a man in a brown uniform strolled into the room.

He held an electronic device and punched in some information. "Good afternoon."

Too stunned to speak, she set her purse down and signed the digital screen.

"Have a great one." He handed her the delivery and left.

The return address was "Katz and Associates, LLC." She ripped the paper and pulled out the letter and a small envelope marked "For Rachel."

The attorney stated he'd come across the document in her mother's safe deposit box. She admired the familiar rendition of her name before opening the note.

Rachel skimmed the words and zeroed in on the crux of the message.

Perhaps you will understand this reoccurring dream.

A dark shadow flies to me, flaunting a silver ring with a ruby or garnet and symbols marked on the sides. I have no such ring, nor have I seen it, but the shadow always whispers your name. Whenever I stared into that old mirror, I thought about how that ring must have some kind of power. I know it sounds silly, but I've always thought the mirror was alive—it's made me wonder who in our family acquired it and where it came from.

Anyway, I can rest, knowing I have told you. I wish you a long happy life and hope to see you again, my dearest.

Love always, Mom.

Rachel sat on top of her desk, her hands crunching the letter in her lap. Her thoughts raced about Wilcox and the ring. A terrible idea popped into her head, but her mind was made up. It was the only way to put an end to her madness.

A row of pregnant women slumped on a dirt floor, manacles cinching their arms and legs, darkness shrouding them. The cave emanated the most profound despair. Rachel couldn't look away. One of the women clawed her own face, her cheeks shredding as she scraped, chunks of flesh dropping onto her chest. Her breasts were already gouged, blood dripping from gaping wounds. Milk dribbled from her nipples. The white and crimson streams ran down her nakedness, rolling along her swollen belly. The mother next to her ripped out fistfuls of hair as she wailed in unimaginable anguish.

Infants screeched like prehistoric birds. Amid it all, a man finished thrusting into one of the women he pinned to the wall. Her head hung, her face wet with tears. He pushed off her, letting her fall to the ground.

His black eyes found Rachel's. She looked away, noticing a teenage boy, his back pressed against the wall. His eyelids were shut tight and his mouth twisted and puckered, just like John did when flustered. "Some protégé," Master barked.

Her snoring had woken her up before, but had never screamed herself awake. Gasping for air, Rachel dashed from the bed and gripped the toilet seat, dry heaving into the bowl.

Rachel's mind was numb as she drove to her office.

Turning the key in the door, she noted the scraps of gel polish clinging to her nails. One of her jagged fingernails snagged her dress as she teetered into the room. She caught a glimpse of her make-up free face in the mirror as she passed. Her hair was only a slightly neater version of bed head. Rubbing her tongue across her teeth, she realized she'd forgotten to brush. She swished a swig of water and swallowed. After spraying herself with perfume, she set the bottle of Zephyrhills on the side table.

Tapping her foot, she watched the digital clock on the wall. He'd arrive any minute.

Once the outer door sounded, she rushed to let him in.

"Mr. Wilcox, thanks for coming in." She waved him across the threshold.

"Any excuse to see you." He winked. "I like your new look, by the way. Sexy."

"Have a seat." She fumbled through the papers on her desk. "It's here somewhere."

"A little unprepared today, huh?"

Pulling the desk drawers open, she rummaged through the folders. "I just had it."

He studied her every move.

"Here it is." After whipping the form from the file, she passed it to him.

"Pretty sure I signed this one already." He tilted his head while taking the pen from her.

"If you did, it's not in your file." Lying was not one of her talents. "Your caseworker is going to be checking in. I'd hate for all the ducks not to be in a row."

Smacking his lips, he autographed the form.

Rachel glimpsed the bottle on the table. He'd usually have opened it by now. "This might be a good time to address your flirtations."

He laughed. "Who, me?"

"You know exactly what I'm talking about."

Leaning back, he patted his hands on his thighs. "Does it bother you?"

"That's not the issue here, Mr. Wilcox. The issue is that I'm here to help you as your *therapist*. I'm calling this to your attention so we can continue a professional relationship. It also gives you the opportunity to correct your behavior."

"And if I don't?"

The lack of sleep and her shot nerves were wearing away her filter. She wanted desperately to swear at him. "You know the answer to that."

"Okay, I'll behave, doc." He smirked as if they just had sex. All the vivid positions of their intertwined bodies probably reeled through his mind.

She tightened her teeth, fanning herself with the file folder. There was a flash of him getting up, seizing her by the arms, and kissing her passionately. Her body surrendered as if it was happening in real time.

He uncapped the Zephyrhills and drank, watching her cheeks flush.

Discovering some gum from her desk drawer, she popped a piece in her mouth. Soon she was chewing it like she was Olivia Newton John in her hot pants, a shred of her feminine power emerging.

"Well...I-I t-think I-I-I'll be going, d-doc."

She pushed back in her chair, mentally thanking one of her addict clients for mentioning where he met his dealer. It had come in pretty handy last night when she scored the GHB. She was half-ashamed of herself for stooping so low and half-proud of the balls she had mustered.

Wilcox's eyes lost their bad boy fierceness. His head bobbed as he struggled to stay conscious. He jerked to alertness. "What the f-f-fuck have y-y-yo-o-ou done?"

Rachel rose and approached him. "Who, *me*?" she asked in a mocking tone.

He tried to get to his feet, but he plopped back into his chair. His lips moved, but no words came out. After swaying back and forth, he collapsed, arms dangling to the floor and drool pooling at the corners of his mouth.

Rachel picked up his hand and regarded the ring. She had to twist and finagle it from his finger. All the while she watched his face to make sure he didn't wake.

Once the ring was in her palm, she breathed easier. Slipping the silver piece on her forefinger, she was surprised at how perfectly it sat there. Admiring the red stone gleamed in the lamplight, it seemed as if the jewelry had always been hers.

Her vulnerability faded, and an intense determination replaced it. As she kicked off her heels and confronted the mirror, she sensed it bending to her will. The surface stirred as if a finger dipped into the liquid glass. Her reflection rippled, her blue eyes turning the color of the deep ocean, almost black. Not waiting for an unseen hand, Rachel boldly stepped through the pervious barrier leading to the other side.

In the tent's glow, he slept peacefully on the mattress. Rachel gingerly slipped the ring from his finger as he stirred.

His eyelids opened, revealing a gentleness there. Although still familiar, his eyes were a light hazel. While climbing onto him, she put the ring on, smiling to herself.

He appeared startled, but didn't protest as Rachel bent down to kiss him. His lips were eager for hers as he grabbed ahold of her hips. The bond between them, whatever it was, coursed within her. For a moment they seemed as equals— finally, it was happening. She allowed herself to embrace the sensation as her body awakened, so alive, so aroused, like never before.

Any residual guilt and shame melted away. The victim energy disintegrated. She had come back here to end the nightmares, to end the infanticide. She was terminating the suffering of all the breeders and the life they spawned. Then she'd be healed, and maybe by proxy, so would Ashley and Wilcox. No more powerlessness. Her soul independent and whole—her own inner child safe at long last.

These noble ideas ebbed and flowed. She rolled onto her side, drawing her lover to her. The dark shadow she'd encountered awhile before had materialized in the center of the tent, suspended above them, its eyes burning like flames. The face was a black skull. Its talons unfurled in wisps, one pointing to the mirror.

You can end it all. Kill him. It's the only way.

That was like murdering herself. As she continued to kiss the man in her arms, she no longer feared him. But she knew not to trust the shadow. She closed her eyes, ignoring its urging.

A gust of air blew against her face. The skull's flaming glare was only inches from her as it floated at her lover's back.

Wilcox has woken. He knows what you've done.

She didn't care what happened on the other side of the mirror. The ring was here. It was on *her* finger. What did it matter what took place in the present? She was righting the wrongs in the here and now.

Ah, but if this one goes back there. That'll change everything.

What did that even mean? Suddenly fear prickled in her belly as the shadow dissolved into the body of the man with her on the bed. His eyes turned black. A frightening anger roused in him as he shoved her aside. The force sent her tumbling from the mattress and onto the ground.

He went for the mirror, the glass twinkling with warm candlelight.

She scrambled to her feet and searched for a heavy object—any heavy object.

Closer and closer to the portal he marched, his hand beckoning to the reflection. His intent expression was accented by the slightest grin—one that indicated a plan.

Rachel lunged for the pewter cup next to the wine. With all the force she could muster, she launched it at the mirror. The image of the man surrounded by the golden light shattered as the shards of glass clinked to the floor. While the shadow left her lover's body and dissipated amid the broken fragments, he toppled lifelessly to the ground.

She sank to her knees. Putting her hands to her face.

There was no going back.

A servant boy held a silver bowl. Rachel's thick chestnut tresses pooled over her shoulders. Eyes black as midnight looked back at her from the surface of the water as she wet a cloth and cleaned her face and neck.

Any recollection of her life as a therapist or a man named Wilcox somewhere in another time and place was erased.

"Bring him to me," she said forcefully, beaming with expectancy.

The boy bowed. After a few minutes, he tugged the leash of a collared man. The captive's hazel eyes studied the floor as he obediently trudged along.

Rachel loosened her ebony robe while sauntering to the mattress that lay between them. "Look at me," she barked.

He hesitated, so she reached for his chin and lifted it.

"I said look at *me*."

He finally did as she commanded. "Yes, Master."

They had taken her purse, her hat and gloves, and made her surrender her jewelry.

"It's for your safety, Ms. Rachel," the nurse with emerald-colored eyes said. "You follow the rules and you might just get out of here—just in time to fulfill a *great destiny*." She plopped a few pills into a tiny paper cup.

Rachel considered the consequences of telling the woman to fuck off. That's what she really wanted to do, but she was in enough trouble already.

"We all have one, you know." The nurse adjusted the pins on her cap.

Rachel chased the pills down with water, studying the linoleum.

"A destiny," she said, as if Rachel cared.

"Oh." Rachel's face was devoid of expression.

Smacking her gum, the nurse regarded Rachel's face. "Weird. Something about you is so familiar."

Rachel dispatched a look of irritation, rolling her eyes.

In a daze Rachel followed a waddling orderly, who puffed on a cigarette, down a sterile white hallway and through the communal room. A female patient swayed to Jo Stafford's "You Belong to Me" crooning from the radio. *Maybe you'll be lonesome too...and blue...* The same song had played when Rachel and Johnny were in her basement. His lips contorted nervously as she, wearing only her Bobby socks, shoved him back on the couch, pinning him by the wrists. Although his eyelids widened in surprise, she felt him through his pants. Having grown bored of his submission, this time she had raised the stakes, wanting to hurt him.

In one of the rooms down the next hallway, a young woman hugged her knees, rocking herself on the bed. Beyond another window, a girl knocked her forehead on the glass, her eyes crossed and her sweaty hair clinging to her scarred cheeks.

Rachel refused to examine the other rooms as they went by. The orderly almost disappeared into the walls in his white smock and pants. Stopping in front of a metal door with a rectangular strip of glass, he handed her a cotton gown and pair of slippers. "Leave your clothes on the bed. I'll be back to take you to your session with the doctor."

Rachel tripped into the cell, the door clanking at her back. She harvested the ring from her bra, admiring the glittering blood red stone in the sunlight shining in from the tiny window above. Rubbing the silver with her thumb, she swiftly tucked it away again before anyone caught her with it.

Then she changed into the gown, folding her pink floral dress at the edge of the bed. Her lividness at being in here riled under waves of giddy euphoria.

She hummed as the orderly returned and led her to an office at the end of the hall.

The doctor behind the desk wasn't the ordinary-looking nerd she'd expected. His short brown hair curled up just above his forehead and she wondered if it was a cowlick or if he intentionally styled it that way. His kind hazel eyes hid behind horned rimmed glasses.

She stood in front of the desk, pulling her gown tight against her womanly figure with one hand. With the other hand, she traced a line from her neck to her décolleté. An eyebrow raised, she projected a feigned innocence.

He averted his eyes. "Please, have a seat."

Wetting her lips, she lowered herself into the chair. "Only since you asked me so *nicely*," she purred.

"Do you know why you are here?" he asked.

She twirled a dirty blonde lock around her finger. "I'm sure you'll remind me."

His brow wrinkled while he jotted something down. Perspiration dotted his temples. "Tell me about the neighbor boy—about the restraints."

She bit her lip, remembering Johnny writhing beneath her, not asking her to stop. She examined the therapist's mouth, wondering what he'd taste like. Chuckling deviously, the lock of hair wound even tighter on her finger. "Oh, that?"

"Yes *that*. That has your father in a very serious pickle. Do you understand the gravity of this?" He pushed the bridge of his glasses and ran his hand through the side of his hair.

"I understand *lots* of things, doc." Rachel leaned forward, the V-necked gown revealing her ample cleavage.

The therapist didn't peek, but she knew he took in the sight in his peripheral vision.

"I see." He adjusted his glasses. "Like that you could be pregnant?"

"Why—because we're all just baby machines, is that it?" She bit her lip, the drugs stripping away her filter.

"It's not that simple."

"Isn't it? My mother cooks and cleans in a dress and high heels. That's not what *I* want. Can you understand that, doc?" She ran her fingers up her thigh, gradually peeling back the gown.

He got up to open the window.

"It *is* getting hot in here." Turning to the gilded mirror to her right, she admired his ass in the reflection. The daylight beamed around him, making him angel-like. She grinned devilishly to herself, fishing the ring from her bra and enclosing it in her palm.

A deep sigh exhaled from his lungs. "We must work on redirecting the tide of your soul. You're on a slippery slope—but it *can* be corrected." He spun around in a daze, watching something in the mirror.

The ring now on Rachel's finger, she played with it.

Seemingly in a trance, the therapist paced toward his reflection, his hand outstretched...

THE RECLUSE

JOHN BODEN

—She types with her head down, bowing like a monk. The pallid glow from the monitor paints her face white. She is a china doll. Her fingers dance- *clickity-click* over the keys. Information flutters invisibly through the air over our heads. I watch her and listen and silently swoon. The air kicks on and makes the calendars and notes taped to cubicle walls flutter and whisper like batwings. The ductwork sighs cool.

—The girl has been gone for at least an hour. I sit there and stare at my computer. The cursor blinking at me, cussing and degrading my lack of courage. "Pussy," it taunts, "You could have gone to her, walked right up to her and spoken." Guilty as I had not. I chew another hangnail and suck the blood and sigh. The cursor keeps baiting me. "Fuck you," I sneer as I turn it off. I pinch the bridge of my nose until spots dance before my tired eyes. A tear of sweat rolls down my forehead.

—I go to her cube and sit in her chair. I touch her pens and pencils. I smell her box of tissues and smile at the candid pictures of her and her friends. Her stupid cat. Washed out comic strips taped to the wall panel. I had almost forgotten about Ziggy. My chest feels as though it could explode at any second. My sternum creaks, as though all the feelings I have for her will break free. And if that happens, all the ugliness I've held inside would seek freedom as well. Thick, squirming tendrils of bile black and seething rage. Disdain and disgust dripping from the tips of twitching tentacles. I lay my glasses on her desk, perspiration trickling from black plastic and staining the blotter. I rub my aching head. My stomach grumbles and sends an urgent burn up the back of my throat. This is love.

—The following day, she comes in early. I am at my desk, actually I never left. I washed myself in the restroom sink and put on a spare shirt that I keep in my drawer. The wrinkles hide behind the pinstripes. She smiles as she walks by and something cracks below my breastbone. I look at her and smile back. "Hi," I attempt, but the feeble thing gets lost in the air, a mote of dust in a storm. She goes down the row and disappears behind her wall. I roll my chair to the desk and turn on the monitor. Cursor says "Good morning, Coward" and I flick it off. My fingers ache and I stretch and flex them. They crackle like flames. "Do it," I goad myself. I get up and walk the row like a condemned man.

—"Emily," I say as I round the corner. She turns smiling and I smile and raise the hand that holds the string. The invisible string that holds back the myriad. All the love and hate. All the anger and awe. All the seedy inner workings. She sees it is me and the smile falters. A little, but enough to break the string. Deep inside there is a snap and a growl. A snarl that swells and grows and I feel suddenly tight. This is how it always plays out for me. Always. Déjà vu and lazy eight.

—I cry as I unbutton my shirt and barely get it off before the maw gnashes and barks. The saliva foams. The tongues waggle and pull her in. A hundred and seventeen teeth grind and eradicate. She is devoured and I am alone. I stand statue still for minutes that seem like days. Slowly, I button the shirt and look around at her cubicle. The clock says it is nearly seven. I have a few minutes to clean up and get to my desk before anyone else shows up. I sit quietly all morning. No one notices Emily's void. No one notices anything different. No one notices me. Just like any other day.

—Maybe the next girl will be the one, maybe I can just say hello.

DOG TIRED

EDDIE GENEROUS

"You can't fall asleep. Come on, Babe."

Prince's voice shook the moment's drowsiness into acknowledgement. Cassandra had been tipping ever closer to that abyss, skull bobbing on a loose neck, shaggy black hair dancing before her face. Quickly, as if caught with finger s in the cookie jar, she snapped her neck straight, drew back her lids, and opened the glovebox.

The wound on her arm refused to heal. It gaped, a weepy pink valley of pain. Wrapping it did not help. Besides, giving it air didn't hurt it. She could look at it as a reminder when sleep attempted to steal her away.

"They don't kick the same after a while, huh?" she asked and popped two little blue pills, recapped the orange pharma bottle, and stuffed it in with the other head altering assistants dwelling within the glovebox.

Prince sniffed. His nose had been runny for three days. It got that way when he didn't sleep. Not sleeping made his eyes go funny, too. While he drove, he saw beasts in every corner of the world ready to leap out onto the blacktop and destroy their final vestiges of hope.

A few of those beasts might've been real.

The beginning seemed like a lifetime ago. It was a perfect night. The half-moon glowed yellow. T-shirt weather clung to world like static, in spite of the date on the calendar. Love was on the air. Their ears rang from the Chemical Overpass concert, the thumps, the electric guitars, that unwholesome but wholly welcome rhythm. The block was dim. A few lights along the street were out and city workers were perpetually busy elsewhere.

There were reports, always elsewhere, of sick people running rampant.

That was then.

"We have to stay awake. Come on, please."

Prince leaned up against Cassandra seconds before perfection ceased.

Her breath had been hot in his ear as her body agreed with the goal of his body. His lips sucked at her collarbone. Her hand dug at the button of his jeans. His right index finger and middle finger rubbing at the fleshy bulb hidden amid moist flaps. Her hips jerked at his touch.

The button came open and she grasped his bulging penis. Prince inhaled a deep breath. Cassandra moaned once with pleasure, and then screamed with surprised pain.

Prince tensed, jarred by the impending climax.

From the shadows next to their doorway, a woman, dishevelled and sopping wet, burst forth. The harried figure latched onto Cassandra with a wide mouth of jagged teeth. A scream rose as fangs broke flesh. Enraged, Prince punched at the figure threatening to repeat the injury, her frothy mouth stretched, while Cassandra pawed the door open. The woman fell after Prince's third shot, stumbling over a broken skateboard left behind by one of the kids from the third floor apartments.

That night, Cassandra had begged to take a nap as she poked at the gaping wound, as if she hadn't been listening to the news all week, as if she was somehow immune to the world. Prince stared into her eyes, doing his damnedest to avoid thinking about the deep scratches dug into his flesh, and said, "Babe, no."

"Only like a day or two more before this is over, right?" Cassandra asked.

"Hope so."

"Can't be more than that, can it?"

This is a question for the gods. Prince was far from a god. Prince was man thirty-nine-years-old, driving a stolen Oldsmobile Alero across the country trying to beat time. He was a man in the same T-shirt and jeans he wore to that Chemical Overpass show nine days earlier.

The stolen car reeked of mingled sweat, chocolate milk, the watered down motor oil scent of empty Red Bull cans, and the KFC they'd collected by waving a desperate machete at four late-night high school dropouts being pretty much all there was left to be for their particular ilk.

"Do you love me?" Prince asked. It sounded romantic, a Bonny and Clyde kind of affair, but really, he was thinking about that old Meat Loaf song, wondering if it could *actually* get any easier to be there until a final act.

"I love you long time," Cassandra said, a phrase she'd intoned dozens of times jokingly, without humor in her tone, gazing out onto the auburn world of dust and dead trees.

Folks were not happy about Prince and Cassandra when Prince stepped out of prison and whisked away the nineteen-year-old waitress saving up for a hotel management course at Bell College. Cassandra's father forbade her leave and she made tracks all the quicker for it.

Romeo and Juliet, baby. Do parents never learn?

Then again, does fresh love never learn?

Prince wasn't such a bad guy, she'd told her friends. Prince's wife, Lena, had waited for him while he did his time, raising their spawn and casting aside the need to keep up any attractiveness. Marriage was a guarantee and there weren't supposed to be options for an ex-con—*them's the breaks*.

Parole Officer Wilma Jacobs had arranged for Prince to be a custodian at a local theatre complex. It was there that he met Cassandra. It was there that his rugged facial features and prison-hard physique tempted the younger woman. It was there that the sparks first flew.

Prince had donned jeans and a tight-fitting Beck t-shirt. It was cool in a throwback kind of vibe. He'd purchased it when the world loved a *Loser* and had worn it three years before relocating to the clink for a six to ten stint.

Overcrowding, good behavior, and recognition of excessive sentencing traits of a certain judge sent the former failed stick-up man free from his punishment. Clean slate, a job paying minimum wage, and an obese wife with three rotten kids that acted as if they wanted all the smacks they got.

He accepted the party address. It only made sense that Prince should want to blow off from the digs for a night with a six-pack, two little MDMA pills, and a mind to touch something pretty.

Back then, they burned with passion. The passion remained, but it shifted. There was no choice but to let it shift.

"How much do you love me?" Cassandra asked. She yawned and slapped her face twice. Hard.

Prince gave a sideways glance. Even sleep-deprived and dishevelled, she was the coal that burned at his core. "Cas, I'm only doing this 'cause you make it worthwhile. I don't go on without you. That's how much I love you."

"You're such a sweetheart." She yawned. "Where do you think we'd be right now if we'd stayed home from Chemical Overpass?"

Zillion-dollar question there. The kind of things daydreams thrive on, like knowing the lotto numbers an hour before the call, ticket in hand bought and paid for.

"Don't know. Grab me another can, huh?"

Cassandra nodded and fished a tallboy of sugar-free Monster Energy from the discarded empties around her feet. The switch to sugar-free occurred at the last Texaco they'd pillaged because they needed a conquerable enemy. The little battles. They'd assured each other that it was the sugar and not all the other stuff that gave them migraines and made them barf high-octane soup all over the interior of the Olds.

"Crack it, huh? My fingers are, like, glued," he said and laughed nervously. His digits had cramped in a steering wheel grip. The trick was to keep moving, eastbound to catch more tomorrows sooner. Even an hour might change the world. "Thanks." He accepted the open can and sipped.

"If we get through this, I'm never drinking another drop of this shit in my life. Coffee neither," Cassandra said.

Thinking ahead was good. Thinking ahead was hope.

When they first hit it off, before the spree or the Chemical Overpass show, they lived in a bachelor apartment in Olympia. Prince wasn't supposed to leave the city, but his P.O. warmed and agreed to keep quiet since he'd been a model parolee and this new change was for the positive. At Delphi Trucking Prince was still cleaning, but rigs instead of candy-coated carpets, and for fifty-cents more an hour. Cassandra waited tables at a Golden Corral. They lived stingy with plans for a white picket future and maybe even kids that weren't trash.

Maybe just a dog to start.

Eventually, though. Eventually.

They'd put the payment up for a rundown bungalow, every damn cent they had in the accounts, and Prince felt a pride he'd never known swell in his chest. One week before they were to hold the keys, they went to the Chemical Overpass show, despite all the crazy stuff on the news. The packs. The bite victims. The stuff hard to take seriously. Besides, it was payday and the working life demanded a vent.

Plus, it's common knowledge that the media blows every dinghy into the Titanic. All that stuff about gathering up the injured for testing and slaughtering the infected on sight had to be bull. Who could believe anything the news showed anymore? The shit seemed barnyard deep. The reports about the eyes and the hair were laughable.

Were.

The radio hit static and Prince noticed after a few seconds. He'd become mostly disconnected. A man on the move.

"Hey, Cas?"

He looked at Cassandra, tears streaming down her cheeks. It had happened often since they'd started out. This was the longest he'd seen her go without makeup.

"I can't do it. It almost seems better just to sleep, you know? You know?"

"Cas, no. Find us a station, some pop shit we can sing along to."

Radio stations had grown fewer and too often nasally radio news heads bogarted the airwaves. Before, people didn't believe what they heard. People couldn't really take it seriously. Not until they had to, then the phrase *don't fall asleep* became life.

"Recent updates confirm the early reports. A joint study underway in the Canadian Arctic suggests that the shifting lunar cycle can be blocked by natural sunlight as the..."

"We should be going north," Cassandra said, tears drying on her beleaguered face.

"Don't think we'd make it across the border. Find us some tunes, huh?"

She did. They sang Britney and Abba and Bowie and Red Hot Chili Peppers. Hours passed and the fuel needle fell past E. The red light flaring, Prince pulled into a quiet Shell station with a car rental office located on the side. The lights were bright. There was a bus stop sign next to the highway, rusty and birdshot pocked. Down an asphalt path running behind the Shell was a tiny train station.

"Pretty quiet," Prince said, the hairs on the back of his neck prickling. "Grab the shooter, maybe things aren't so good."

"Let's go on then," Cassandra said.

The gas gage told the story of choices lacking. Besides, they'd gathered arms. Things should be easier.

"Babe."

It was a slaughterhouse inside. Blood smeared up walls and bits of meat accented scarlet puddles on the tile floor. The bodies that ought to be there were not there. That was so much worse than finding corpses. Outside, a clamour announced action and instinctively, Cassandra and Prince ducked amid the potato chips and the wiper blades. Hearts rattling like janitor keys. Cassandra's breathes inched toward hyperventilation.

"No, git! Fuck! Fu-aaah!" a voice shouted from outside.

The wet snapping and slopping accompanied a pack of growls. Cassandra leaned to look out onto the parking lot. Six enormous wolves lapped at a blood puddle in between bites of flesh torn from bone.

A whine left Cassandra's mouth. A single wolf lifted its head to consider the lot peripheries. It bent back down to munch only to stop again. It spun around fully this time and Cassandra jumped out of view. The rack behind her bounced, items shimmying toward the tips of their tines.

The gentle click of paws on tarmac approached.

"Cass, Cass, you have to be quiet," Prince whispered.

Cass' breath whipped out of her mouth like hurricane bleats, sounding almost sexual. She squeaked as a warm weight touched her arm and then face.

Prince leaned in, his hand over her mouth, eyes meeting her gaze. "Cass, babe, do you love me?"

Heart slowing, breathes easing, Cass nodded. At the door, the clicks neared and then fell against the glass. Loud snorts of inhalation announced that the wolf suspected something. A paw reared and landed with a horrendous bang against the glass of the door.

The glass cracked. And again. Pieces clanged to the ground.

Prince and Cass embraced one another as if it was to be the last time. Tears streamed from four eyes as if they shared a single set of ducts.

More glass fell. The snorting, sniffing mongrel inched its snout within, paw crunching through fallen glass.

Far away, a wolf howled.

The nearby sniffing ceased moving...then resumed.

Two wolves howled then, both in the distance.

The sniffing hitched.

The paws prattled away.

Prince and Cass remained a statue until the adrenaline that had stiffened their bodies melted away and they softened.

"Load up. Come on," Prince said.

The news outlets had used words like packs and roaming. Again, some things really don't sink until they're there in full color and texture, growling, snarling, snapping, and you feel that blood trickling.

"Quiet, get what we need and we'll take a rental," Prince whispered. "Come on, faster, load up."

The rental smelled fresh and wonderful. For a few minutes, Prince drove like a Sunday man skipping church to drink in the real glory of a day off work. The radio lowered and Prince came back around to the exhausted plight that had become his existence.

Cassandra stiffened. A hand latched onto Prince's forearm. He shot her a look.

"Listen," Cassandra said, voice tremoring.

Prince opened his mouth to ask and then snapped it closed.

As gently and quietly as was possible, Prince wheeled the roomy Ford Escape to the shoulder. It was nearly black outside and he was all jitters, coming down again. Too much of a good thing wears and soon that good thing can't compete with a bad thing.

Prince looked at Cassandra. Her eyes had massive bluish bags beneath them. They were wide with fright. At least a good scare can raise the heartrate. A safe scare. Scared is good for staying awake.

But this? This was a bad scare.

Still, same result.

Hearts pounded.

There was somebody or something snoring in the cargo hold of the vehicle. It was an enviable sound. It was a terrifying sound. No regular sleep would withstand a carjacking.

"This is bad," Cassandra whispered. "Should we run?"

"On foot? No," Prince snapped, thinking.

"Please don't. I can't. I can't." Cassandra shook her head, sweat matted hair moving very little.

"I know... Do you love me?"

She nodded, eyes closed.

"Open your eyes, Cas. You're gonna get behind the wheel. I'm gonna open the hatch."

Cassandra grimaced.

"If it's already... If it's already... I'll scream and then shoot it, but I can't shoot it in the back, I'll hit the gas tank and we won't get anywhere with fuel leaking. After I shoot it, I'll get in the back before it has its head on straight. If it's not already...changed, I won't shoot. I'll get it out and jump in, then you drive. Got it?"

"I can't leave you."

"Cas, do you love me?"

Cassandra nodded emphatically, childishly.

Prince wanted to wrap her up and take her away from everything. He couldn't imagine a self not connected to this woman. If there is a god, it lives in the light her smile shines.

"Love me and do as I say."

Prince reached back for the rifle and exited the vehicle. Cassandra climbed over the center console and got behind the wheel.

Fingers pressed against the handle, Prince counted twenty good breaths, nerving himself, imagining all the horrors that might be behind the door. Paused. A fresh terror encompassed his world. What lay behind the door was in with Cassandra. This gave him all the strength that he needed to act.

The hatch swung upwards. There was was a bundled figure. The blood pooled around a cotton-covered nub. The figure had lost a hand. Lost it viciously most likely. Prince lifted his eyes to meet Cassandra's in the rearview. It was a moment's glance. Eyes fell back onto the stowaway.

As if unravelling before an audience, the figure stretched. It was a boy and his breathing changed as his lids snapped open. Golden and shimmery, those irises glowed the truth of the matter. The injury was no accident. The boy had been bitten. A monster had stolen his hand. Instantly upon waking, the changes darkened the boy's flesh with a coat of incredibly coarse fur. This boy bore the infection and was about to wear it like a fresh new birthday suit.

It was like the woman outside the apartment building. Prince thought it was a fur coat at first. After the bite and the scratch, what the news said rang a million truths.

This boy was a monster as was that woman, and as those beasts in gas station lot were. Quickly, Prince tossed the shotgun into the backseat, grabbed onto the boy and yanked him out of the cargo hold while it continued the brief metamorphosis. The boy landed in a cloud of dust and snapped a slobbery jaw, fully formed in the matter of three heartbeats.

"Drive!" Prince screeched as he leapt over the ravenous canine figure.

Prince felt a mouth land on his steel-toed boot as Cassandra stamped the gas, sending dust and gravel shooting out in their wake. The wolf that was once a small boy chased after the vehicle in a race he'd never match once Cassandra hit forty miles an hour.

"Tell me you're ok!" Cassandra shouted.

Prince had been watching the world through the open hatch door. Lost in the motion.

"Stop, I'll close this then come up there."

"Oh thank god. I can't. I can't drive!" she wailed.

The pain in her voice was awful. It had only been worse when it was still new. Back then, the news still called the infected people *men* and *women*. Those who witnessed the infected and managed to get away unscathed had a more colloquial name for them, a silly name, an impossible name, the only befitting name: Werewolf.

You've got to see one to believe one.

Night was full and the moon was high outside the window. Prince stared forward, losing himself again in the yellow lines dancing up the middle highway and the shapes jutting from corners beyond the headlamp reach.

"Cas, do you love me?" he asked.

There was no answer.

"Cas?" Prince turned to face her.

Outside their apartment after the show, the werewolf bit Cassandra on the arm and scratched a mean groove into

Prince's shoulder before Prince stabbed out with three prison-yard perfected jabs. Even nine days earlier, there were lunar cycle theories. If you stayed awake long enough, the infection passed harmlessly. Twenty-five days was a tall order, if the bite came at the beginning of the cycle. The scientists were miles behind understanding this thing and how it came to exist.

Prince and Cassandra met infection well after the halfway point of the assumed lunar cycle.

There was a possibility.

There was a chance.

Love and will, baby.

Love is worth fighting for, always was and always will be. They could drive until the end of time.

"Cas?" Prince whispered, jaw line protruding at his bristled cheeks as he ground his teeth.

Cassandra snored gently, head leaning against the window.

He had choices. There was a possibility that he might yank open the door, pull her out, and be on his way. Unlikely. There was also the rifle. A single shot to her sleeping head would do it, no questions.

"Why?" Prince whispered and pulled the Ford to the shoulder.

He closed his eyes and waited, wired and lapping against a sleepy shore, but never quite beaching. Fraught mind wandering, he thought of his life in two parts.

Loser. Lover.

Loser. Lover.

A groan of self-pity and undeniable agony left his tight lips.

The snoring ceased. If she awoke before he slept... Prince peeked out his right eye.

Drool ran down Cassandra's jaw, dangling from the coarse grey fur. Her gaze seared glowing spots into his re-closed eye like sparklers on a July night. Her shirt had stretched and her arms had lengthened into skinny legs. Talon-like claws jutted from each fingertip.

"Please, Cas. Let me fall asleep. I'll sleep and we'll do this one togeth—"

HARDENED HEARTS

THE PINK BALLOON

TOM DEADY

"Daddy can't go." Grace's eyes were full of unshed tears. "He promised."

Mary closed her eyes and took a long breath. "What do you mean? Is Daddy sick, honey?"

Grace shrugged and finally a tear slipped out and ran down her face.

"You sit with Brian for a minute and I'll talk to him, okay?" She plastered a smile on her face and left the room without waiting for an answer. Mary found him still in bed.

"What the hell are you doing, Dave? Grace has been waiting all week for the fair."

Dave sat up in bed rubbing his eyes. "Babe, I'm sorry, I forgot..."

"You forgot?" Mary closed the bedroom door so Grace wouldn't hear. "You forgot a promise you made to your six-year-old daughter?" Her voice bordered on a yell.

Dave stared at her shaking his head. "I had a hell week at work. You do realize it's my job that keeps the roof..."

"Don't you dare play the breadwinner card, Dave Malloy. I put my career on hold to start a family, not to be a single parent. You need to be here for Grace and Brian even if you're not here for me." Her voice softened, "We have everything we need. Just come, please?"

Dave sighed. "I'm exhausted, Mary. Johnson's been riding me about..."

Mary cut him off. "Forget it, Dave." Her tone was deflated and it came out as a whisper. She didn't know if she meant the fair or the whole damn marriage. She left the room, closing the door quietly behind her.

Mary pushed the carriage along the crowded sidewalk, blowing an errant piece of hair out of her face. "Keep one hand on the stroller, honey, like we talked about." Grace smiled at her, making everything better.

"Thanks for taking me to the fair, Mommy."

Mary smiled back. "Thanks for being such a good helper with the baby." A silly gurgle came from the depths of the stroller as if in agreement. She glanced at Brian but he had already fallen back asleep. Despite being with her children on a packed street, a cloak of loneliness settled on her. *Why couldn't Dave be here with us? Why was he always working for that next big thing when days like today were what mattered?* When she looked up, Grace was not holding the stroller. Mary didn't see her at all.

Mary's lungs refused to take in air as panic seized control of her. She whipped her head back and forth but all she saw were unintelligible shapes and random colors. Where was Grace? She tried calling her daughter's name but what came out was a strangled bark. A wave of dizziness washed over her and she gripped the handle of the stroller tightly to steady herself. And there was Grace, not ten feet away with both palms pressed against the drug store window looking at stuffed animals.

"Mommy, can I get a baby elephant?"

Mary gulped in ragged breaths, feeding her brain with oxygen that narrowly prevented her from fainting. On rubbery legs, she pushed the carriage to her daughter. "Not now, honey, let's keep walking. Hand on the stroller, right?" Her voice sounded like it was coming from miles away but Grace didn't seem to notice.

"Sorry, Mommy, hand on the carriage, see?"

That smile, Mary thought, *God help the boys in this town ten years from now*. Her heartbeat had settled back to normal and she began walking.

The Littlefield Fair was an annual tradition that went back as far as residents could remember. It was held on the last Saturday in June and served as an end-of-school celebration and a kick-off to summer. Main Street and a few connecting streets in the center of town turned into a much smaller, less decadent Mardi Gras festival. People dressed in outrageous costumes while mimes and jugglers performed for the crowds. The air was thick with the aroma of fried dough, hot dogs, and cotton candy. The fair seemed to get bigger and more extravagant each year. There was talk of making it a two-day affair and blocking off the streets downtown to accommodate the number of pedestrians but it never seemed to get beyond talk.

Mary and Grace weaved through the throngs of people while little Brian slept peacefully in his stroller despite the heat of the day and the raucous crowd. Mary relented to Grace's begging and got her a Sno-cone. More of it melted onto the front of Grace's dress than she actually got into her mouth, but she enjoyed the slurpy mess so much it made Mary laugh. Grace marveled at a guy walking on enormous stilts, and a troupe of gymnasts performing jumps and flips that seemed to defy gravity.

The smile slipped from Mary's lips and she felt goose bumps pop up on her arms. She was being watched. She glanced around trying to appear casual but her anxiety was creeping close to fear. "Make sure you stick close, Gracie, keep one hand on the stroller." Her voice sounded strained and Grace gave her a funny look, picking up on her discomfort. Mary made a fuss about checking on the baby and again glanced at the faces in the crowd around her.

Was that man slouched in the doorway staring at her? Why was that teenager wearing a wool cap on such a hot day? There were two women dressed in army fatigues and tank tops whispering to each other and glancing in her direction. The magician surrounded by young children seemed to be looking at Grace as he fashioned balloon animals. Everyone was staring at her with malice.

Mary wasn't prone to paranoia and had never suffered from anxiety. It was something other people were plagued with but not her. This could only mean, to her panic-stricken mind, that something was really wrong. "Come on, Gracie, let's head back to the car."

Grace looked at her with an expression of sadness and confusion. "But mommy, we practically just got here!" Her voice wasn't whiney; she spoke matter-of-factly without a hint of childish petulance.

Mary was torn. She loathed disappointing her daughter. That's Dave's job, she thought with a flash of anger. The idea of her husband not wanting to share an event like this with his family infuriated her and saddened her in equal measures. Grace hadn't even bothered to beg Dave to come, knowing it was futile. Mary's fury overrode her tension. "You're right, honey. Come on, there's a guy selling balloons." Grace smiled up at her, and just like that, the world was right again.

An hour later both Mary and Grace were sopping in sweat and exhausted. They'd walked up and down Main Street more times than Mary could count. They stopped in the shade of the massive oak tree on the town common so Mary could feed and change Brian. As much fun as mother and daughter were having, there were several times Mary had the feeling someone was staring at her, following her, but she could never catch anyone. She tried to laugh it off, or blame it on the animosity she was feeling toward Dave, but it didn't stop her from being watchful. "One more trip up and down the street then we're calling it a day, deal?"

Grace clung to the string tethered to her balloon and nodded. Mary had suggested tying the string to the handle of the stroller but Grace wasn't having it. She diligently held the string with one hand and kept the other on the baby carriage. A fire engine rolled slowly by on the street, gaily decorated in bunting and streamers, two firemen waving from the truck.

"Mommy, there's Riley!" Grace had taken her hand off the stroller to point out her friend but quickly put it back, glancing sheepishly at her mother.

Mary waved at Joan Burke, Riley's mom. They had met through their children but quickly realized they had a lot in common and had become close friends. The two women began chatting while their daughters breathlessly exchanged stories of what they had seen at the festival. Mary and Joan commiserated about their husbands not being with them.

Joan sighed deeply. "Steve is home watching the ball game and getting drunk." She tried to keep her tone light but Mary saw the pain in her eyes.

Mary nodded. "Dave said he was going to do yard work but I'm betting he's had a few beers himself and is sound asleep on the couch." A flicker of movement caught her eye.

"Mommy, the clown is giving away candy!" And then she was gone.

Dave watched the clouds float by against the crystal blue backdrop of the sky through half-open eyes. The argument with Mary had already lost its edge, dulled by the knowledge that it wasn't the first fight and wouldn't be the last. He'd make it up to her and Grace. If he made his numbers and got his bonus, maybe they'd be able to pay off the cars and take a real vacation next summer. Missing one silly fair was a small price to pay.

He needed today to re-energize. It was one of those early summer days that made you wish you were a kid again. Because when you were a kid, every summer day was like this and you really didn't have a care in the world. He sipped a beer, ignoring the fact that it was getting warm. Nothing could ruin his mood. Somewhere in the distance a dog barked and old man Dixon started his lawn mower across the street. A lazy smile pulled at the corners of Dave's mouth. That crazy old bird mowed his lawn every day from April through October, he thought. Then he glanced at his own overgrown grass with a pang of guilt. One more beer and I'm all over that lawn.

Something caught his gaze floating against the azure sky. A pink balloon drifted upward in the gentle breeze. Just before

Dave closed his eyes, he heard the faint sound of sirens in the distance.

Dave woke to the same sounds he had dozed off to—sirens. They were closer now, but in his sleepy haze he didn't realize they were right down the street. The sun had made its way around the big oak so that he was no longer in the shade. He blinked stupidly at the sky. How long had he been asleep?

He reached for his cell phone and saw the screen full of missed calls. Before he could check his messages, the sirens grew deafening and flashing blue lights stole his attention as two police cars skidded to a stop in the driveway. He was either too sleepy or too buzzed from the beers to feel anything more than curiosity.

A lanky officer unfolded himself from the driver's seat of the first cruiser, glanced at the second car, and began walking slowly toward him. Dave got up and started moving to meet him when the passenger door the second car opened and stopped him in his tracks. Mary practically fell out of the car and began running toward her husband. It finally hit Dave that something was wrong. Something bad. Mary shrieked unintelligible cries and then she actually did fall, face planting on the lawn. Dave ran to help her, taking her in his arms and feeling her entire body quivering. "Mary, what...?"

A female officer was suddenly at her side, helping her up.

"Officer, what's going on, what's happened?"

The woman was consoling Mary, leaving Dave standing there feeling foolish and inadequate, and, for some reason, guilty. The woman nodded to the male officer and he cleared his throat and removed his hat. Behind them, a car door closed and another female officer started walking towards them holding a baby. "Brian?" And suddenly it was all too clear. Dave was no longer able to draw a breath and his knees buckled. He landed awkwardly on the grass and rolled onto his back, finally getting air in to his lungs in short choking gasps. "Grace, where's Grace?" His words came out between hitching breaths. But somehow he already knew the answer.

"There's been an accident, Mr. Malloy..."

Dave shook his head back and forth rapidly. "Nonononono, please...." He began hyperventilating and the brightness of the day began to dim, only at the edges first, then closing in like the ending of an old movie fading to black.

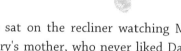

Dave sat on the recliner watching Mary gently rock the baby. Mary's mother, who never liked Dave in the first place, sat next to her shooting angry accusing looks his way. *Why weren't you there? What were you doing that was more important? the look said.* He had no answers other than the errant tear that ran down his cheek.

The police and a heavily sedated Mary had eventually told him what happened. Grace had darted into the street because she saw a clown giving away candy. The driver of the car that hit her was not speeding but simply had no chance to stop in time. The paramedics said she died instantly, as if that made it merciful to anyone.

The driver was a middle-aged man with a spotless driving record, not even a parking violation. He never saw Grace. He was too distracted by the clown on the side of the road He claimed the clown was juggling those giant round lollipops that had colorful swirly designs on them. He also said the clown looked familiar somehow, despite having a painted face.

The thing that confused Dave is that Mary never saw the clown that Grace ran toward. The driver's wife who was in the passenger seat didn't either. The police were asking around but Dave had a weird feeling that they weren't going to find a single person who remembered the clown. His stomach roiled and a sheen of sweat covered his face as he got up and went to the kitchen. With shaking hands, he dialed the Burke's number. Joan answered and the two exchanged awkward words that couldn't come close to meaning anything to either of them.

"Joan, did you or Riley see the clown?" Dave's voice was shaking worse than his hands. He heard the desperation in it. The need for answers he knew he wouldn't find.

"As soon as Grace..." Strangled sobs overtook her and Dave heard the phone drop. He considered hanging up but he had to know. Joan came back after a few minutes, still sniffling but under control. "As soon as Grace ran, Riley and I both looked up. It...it all happened so fast. But... no. There was no clown. I talked to Riley about it... God, Dave, she's devastated. Like the rest of us. But she didn't see it either. There was no clown, Dave."

Dave hung up the phone without responding. A hollowness had seeped into him and he knew it would never leave. He returned to the living room and sat down. He smiled sadly and nodded when Mary and her mom rose to put Brian down for the night. Bitter tears streamed down his face. Mary and her mom would sit in Brian's room watching him sleep, afraid to take their eyes off him.

It's time.

He switched on the television and turned the volume up. With a sigh, he walked through the kitchen and into the garage. It only took a few minutes to cut off a length of garden hose and duct tape it to the exhaust pipe. He sat in the car with the hose sticking in the back window, the lights off, and the engine running, waiting.

Earlier that day he had checked his insurance policy. Mary and Brian would be well taken care of. Better than they would be with him around. Mary would never forgive him just as he would never forgive himself. She was young and beautiful. She would find someone better.

Tears fell relentlessly and he pushed his hands to his eyes, his body wracked with sobs. All he could think of was Grace that morning asking him to come to the fair with her. The disappointment in her eyes when he refused. What man could live with that? There was no way he could kneel in front of her lifeless body and pray to a god he didn't believe in. No way could he watch the tiny casket lowered into the ground and covered with dirt. It made him want to scream. He wanted to close his eyes but feared all he would see was a car striking Grace while he drank beer and napped. He feared it was all he would ever see.

As the fumes began to do their work, his sobs settled to hitching gasps. He felt eerily calm and leaned back. Finally, he did close his eyes. He imagined Grace floating up toward heaven and a beautiful calm washed over him. As he faded away, he pictured a pink balloon drifting upwards in an azure sky.

HARDENED HEARTS

IT'S MY PARTY AND I'LL CRY IF I WANT TO

J.L. KNIGHT

Two weeks had gone by since she died.

Two weeks since time stood still. Two weeks since everything changed. Two unbelievable weeks.

He was still a little stunned. He still hoped it was all a horrible mistake. He knew the hope was a lie.

Their apartment was decorated with streamers and balloons from her birthday party. He sat dully on the couch, looking at the droopy strips of crepe. He remembered the night before her party, how they had blown up the balloons together, laughing, breathless.

He'd gotten lightheaded and she'd blown up most of the balloons.

They hung in colorful clusters in the doorways and corners, round and full. His dim gaze suddenly focused.

He went to their bedroom. He took a safety pin from the little ceramic dish that sat on top of their dresser, among the clutter of lipsticks and change and keys.

Carefully he detached the balloons from the walls. He looked at them thoughtfully as they drifted in a loose airy pile on the floor. He sat down and picked up a pale yellow one, holding it in his hands like a fragile baby.

He opened the pin and made a small hole right next to the knot so it wouldn't pop. Then he gently wiggled the pin, making a little tear.

He raised the balloon to his mouth and inhaled deeply. Her breath filled him. He gulped her air hungrily into his lungs, devouring her. When the pale yellow balloon was an empty shriveled skin, he reached for a rose pink one. And then a sky blue one.

The blue balloon was limp and damp in his hand and he made himself stop. There were nine balloons left. Nine delicate, precious orbs. He gathered them into a plastic garbage bag and put them in the closet.

He rationed them out. They were the most important thing in his life. They lasted six months.

When he hadn't been to work in a few days, the police were notified. They went to his apartment, where they found him sitting in the empty closet, holding a mostly deflated balloon. A woman's face was drawn in black marker on the shrunken latex, now puckered and grossly misshapen. When they tried to take it from him, he began to scream, a high, thin sound, like air escaping from a punctured balloon.

HARDENED HEARTS

CONSUMED
MADHVI RAMANI

We met at a trade fair. Lawnmower salesman, that's me. Serious machinery. Serious business. Serious money. And there are perks. Our lawn was always respectable. Nothing better than riding up and down your yard, going straight along the edges, making everything look perfect.

Yeah, our lawn was perfect. A lawn for barbecues, the chatter of friends through a smoky haze, for sipping glistening glasses of iced tea, eyes closed in the orange warmth, listening to the rustle of birds pecking at the feeder. Then, suddenly they'd startle, and flutter across the smooth green lawn and into the darkness of the woods beyond, as if for no reason at all.

Those woods marked the end of our yard. They weren't too deep though. Sometimes, you'd glimpse a flash of the Thompsons' backyard through the tangle. It was like a shock, that green. Greener, it seemed, than the lawn you were standing on.

Yeah, that was our world. Me and Deb, Cassie and Ben, in our home, surrounded by looming Carolina woods, until the fair. She was at the stand across the aisle. Credit cards, her business. Blue eyes, blonde hair, sharp nose. As soon as I saw her, I knew. Tugged off my wedding band and slipped it into my pocket. It was wrong, but the surge, the tingle, the rush, of breaking free of bounds was refreshing. Besides, I wasn't planning on going further.

Four-wheel steering, zero-turn, 9mph, self-propelled four stoke engine...I threw specifications at visitors, chest puffed. I barely glanced at her, but I could sense her. Her suit, her stockings, the way she moved. I bet she sensed me too; strong, funny, powerful. The visitors must have felt it as well, because I sold more lawnmowers that day than ever before.

Just before closing, I sauntered over. I was pulled, like how when you're on your lawnmower sometimes and you feel like just continuing over into the darkness, taking down all those trees, because you have all of man, all that engineering, that power, that control, beneath you.

Let us make man in our image, after our likeness. And let them have dominion over the fish of the sea and over the birds of the heavens and over every creeping thing that creeps on the earth.

That verse, repeated in the dim, cool church while I stared longingly at the bright day outside, sang in my mind.

"You want a credit card, don't you mister?" she smiled.

"Absolutely," I said, and pulled a form towards me.

Everything flowed like a dream; chatter, laughter, drinks at the hotel bar. Evelyn, her name, recently divorced. I said I was too. Then we were stumbling out the side door for some fresh air and our mouths met, hot and hard, and there, right there, at the edge of the car park—she slid down, undid my pants, and took me into her mouth.

Why did I do it? That's what everyone asks. Marital problems? Mid-life crisis? A moment of madness? No, it was head. But you can't say that to the judge and jury, your kids, your sister, her sister, your neighbors and buddies. That's the truth though. I was hooked from that first night at the hotel carpark. The power. The rush. Like conquering something.

We met at hotels halfway between our homes, went on weekend trips. Sometimes, I drove the distance to her place. And the lies, they kept coming. I was riding high, creating my own landscape. A landscape where I was renovating my house to sell it after divorce. Renovations that made it impossible for her to visit. Was buying a place with her after the sale and living together was the next step.

We started house shopping. It was like a game. At every place, she would try to give me head. We'd loop back and forth, searching, and then—in a closet, a bathroom, kitchen, garage, basement—she'd go down and I'd survey the fixtures, the dustballs, the view from the window, a red ball of energy gathering in my loins, growing hotter and tighter, before... shooting relief.

Deb pointed out the sprouting tufts of weeds in the yard. I snapped. Couldn't she see the pressure I was under? I was attending more conferences, sales-meetings, and trade fairs than ever before. We had bills, expenses, kids in college. I didn't have time for the damn gardening. She stopped asking after that. The grass grew darker, blending with the woods beyond.

Of course, I wasn't attending more conferences, sales-meetings, and trade fairs than ever before. I was meeting Evelyn. Seeing places. Getting head. I told Evelyn that the sale of my house was going through. I couldn't stretch it out any longer. Besides, we had just seen our ideal house.

"We could be moving in by the end of the month," Evelyn said, giddy.

My chest tightened. I needed relief. I pushed her head beneath the sheets, tried to concentrate on the rhythm of her lips, the flick of her tongue, the caress of her breath. How was this going to work out? I couldn't afford another house. And what about Deb, the kids? If I told Evelyn the truth, she would end it. Maybe even tell Deb. I'd lose everything. But how else could I continue the lie? Divorce was expensive.

Evelyn came up, face flushed.

"Hey mister, thought you'd fallen asleep," she said.

"I'm sorry. Just can't stop thinking about the house," I said.

Half-truth, half-lie. Somewhere in between, like the space I occupied. I had driven straight into the woods and the blades had jammed. Soon, Evelyn was asleep, but my brain continued to whirr. There was no way through to the other side, to that bright green future. Then, in the early hours, a spark.

I was an hour and a half away from home. Evelyn was dead to the world. I could make it there and back by six. She would never know I had gone. And the insurance money...

The idea spun, getting stronger, gaining momentum. I sat up, got out of bed, clicked the door shut behind me.

Drove, smooth and steady. Pulled up at the house in the dim blue light. Slipped into the garage and surveyed the cans of gas that had been accumulating there. Crouching mounds of darkness, all in a row. I had a regular delivery of pure, ethanol-free gas, the best kind for keeping the four-stroke engine running at peak performance. They had been piling up since I began my affair with Evelyn. I picked up one, then another, and created a trail, from Deb's SUV, to the pantry and beyond.

Drenched everything. Curtains, carpets, stereos, flat-screens, packets of macaroni cheese, love seats, napkins. The smell was overpowering. I hadn't thought about that. The smell. It was going to wake her up. Wake the neighbors up even. This smell. Unnatural, pungent, seeping into everything. I had to hurry. Went up the stairs. Wardrobes stuffed with the kids' clothes, tables, chairs, duvets, bathmats, baskets of shell-shaped soaps, and finally, the master bedroom.

It was going to wake her. Wake the neighbors even. I hurried upstairs.

The door was ajar. She was snoring on her side. Blocked sinuses. Maybe she wouldn't smell it. Imagine if she did. She'd wake. The panic. What would I say? What would I do? I held my breath, skirted around the room making sure to block the doors and windows and then, I struck the match. The sound of the scrape and the hush of the flame was like a bomb exploding. Her slack face flickered in the darkness. She was just another lump of material blocking my way. I threw down the match, locking the door behind me, retraced my steps, lighting until the cool breeze hit my face. The whiff of lawnmower fuel lingered in my nostrils. I got into the car and pulled away. *Bang!* In the rear view mirror, the house was ablaze. A fizzling explosion of energy.

Ahead, rosy dawn streaked the sky, and I felt relief.

BURNING SAMANTHA

SCOTT HALLAM

She spends twenty minutes stuffing a bra for a chest that will never grow. Not unless she can convince her parents to invest her college savings into hormone therapy or two mounds of silicone.

She peers out her window at the suburban neighborhood lined with maple trees and street lamps illuminating the May evening.

He'll be here any minute, her best friend Andrew.

He agreed to be her date for the spring dance.

As Samantha. Not as what the kids at school call her— Sam. Not as the name her parents gave her the day that she was born with a body that never quite felt right.

Samantha. Not Sam. Not ever again.

She gazes into the mirror, adjusting her neon blue wig. Her hands tremble as she stares back at her carefully-shaven face and lips painted aqua. She tries not to think of the stares she'll receive. She tries to think of slow dancing with Andrew, her head buried in his chest, taking in the smell of his cologne.

He's a little late. Not by much. The dance doesn't start until 7:30. Andrew will be here. That's what matters. Yesterday, he held her hand in the backseat of the school bus.

She pulls at the hem of her little black dress—practices walking back and forth across her room in heels. Straight and tall. She likes how the heels make her calves look.

Samantha hears the growl of an engine. Peering out her bedroom window, she sees Andrew in his father's Camaro. Her flesh shivers and little bumps rise on her arms. She checks her makeup one last time before leaving her bedroom.

She lingers at the top of the stairs as she waits for Andrew to ring the doorbell. Her mother glances up at Samantha, a daughter that her mother never knew she had. She smiles thinly then pretends to tidy up the foyer.

Samantha spies wetness in her mother's eyes. Her dad didn't even bother sticking around. He said that he didn't want to see his faggot son dress up like a slut. He said that he'd be drinking at the bar with this golf buddies and that Sam had better be in bed by the time he got home.

The doorbell rings, and Samantha's stomach clenches. She grips the railing. Her mother opens the door and Andrew walks in wearing a charcoal sports jacket over an electric blue shirt. Tall and lean, a runner's body. His chocolate brown hair cut short. Samantha's hand on the railing becomes wet with perspiration.

He raises his eyes to meet hers, waving a bouquet of flowers in her direction, a spring mix, and flashes that half smile of his. The smile that made Samantha's knees shake the first time she saw him at musical try-outs.

Samantha descends one step at a time, her gaze transfixes on Andrew. When she reaches the bottom, he presents the bouquet to her. She presses her face into the daffodils, peonies, and baby's breath and inhales the fragrance.

She hands the bouquet to her mother who scurries away to the kitchen to put them in water while Andrew and Samantha embrace. She nestles her head underneath his chin and wraps her arms around him. His scent hints at an ocean breeze. She shuts her eyes, the image that has kept her awake at three in the morning for so many nights finally coming true, the image of her and Andrew becoming more than friends.

Her mother returns to the foyer as they separate. Samantha hands her cell phone to her mother, asking for a picture to be taken. She reaches out for the phone, her pasted-on smile crumbles.

Andrew stands beside Samantha with his hands in his pockets and shuffles his feet. She snags his arm and draws herself closer, tells him to smile as Samantha's mother takes a photo.

After a stiff hug from her mother, Samantha takes Andrew by the hand and leads him out to his car. The moon hangs low and bright in the darkening sky, a sky clear and cloudless. He holds the door open for her as she slinks into the passenger seat, flexing her newly-shaven legs, hoping that Andrew will notice. Hoping that his heart skipped a beat when he first saw her tonight on the stairs.

Andrew and Samantha cruise the suburban streets, blaring songs from the screamo bands that they both love, singing along to the soaring harmonies. Andrew has the windows down, the warm night air rushes in as he takes the turns a little too fast. She squeals in delight and playfully slaps him on the shoulder. Who knew that five minutes of small talk after their first musical practice would have led to this night?

They soon pull into the school parking lot outside the gymnasium and shut the engine down, abruptly cutting off the vocalist in mid-shriek. The silence feels heavy as she looks up at the gray concrete building that looms in front of them. She grips the armrest, and for a moment, wonders if she should just call the whole thing off.

Andrew places his hand on hers, his hand warm, and she calms down; her breathing slows. He asks if she's ready for this, asks if she'll slow dance with him.

Samantha stares into his blue eyes — eyes that she's fallen into for months now — and mouths the word "yes."

Andrew, one of the few shades of gray in a school full of black and white. On the track team and a lead in the school musical. Decent grades in Math and English but not good enough to be a labeled a nerd. Somehow, he and Samantha became friends as they hung out during rehearsals and in the back of Mrs. Kendall's trig class. Somehow, he didn't run away when one day after school she spilled her guts over dark-roasted coffee about who she really was.

Even though Samantha asked Andrew to the dance, it was his idea for her to not simply wear a little eyeliner and lipstick, but to go the full mile and wear the wig, the black dress, and the high heels. To show the school, the world that she was Samantha. Not Sam. Not ever again.

Andrew and Samantha get out of the car and walk towards the gymnasium entrance while a few other couples trickle in. As they enter, the throbbing bass and static from the speakers greet them. Already a throng of classmates undulates in the center of the gym. Crystal blue and white streamers dotted with clear and aqua balloons decorate the room. A banner traverses the length of the stage above the DJ equipment displaying the cheesy theme *Frozen in Time*.

They walk hand-in-hand, inching their way towards the dance floor where flashes of red, green, blue, and yellow light bathe the dancers.

Samantha stops at the edge of the crowd, her high heels stuck to the hardwood floor. She's still not sure about any of this, half of her wants to throw caution to the wind and simply dance with the boy of her dreams and swim in the colored lights.

The other half wants to hide in the shadows along the gymnasium wall with the handful of kids without dates, just like she has done during every dance since her Freshman year.

Andrew gently tugs Samantha's arm; she looks up at his grin that melts away the outside world and she's walking again, right into the heart of the dance; the beat pulses with a life of its own, the bass reverberates in her chest and she feels alive in her skin for once, the snickers and sideways glances bounce off her as she dances beside Andrew; Andrew swaying and swinging his arms, offbeat but not caring, their laughter drowns out the shouts of *tranny* and *whore* as if the meathead jocks were speaking a foreign language.

After several up-tempo songs, Samantha asks Andrew to grab her a Coke. He goes to retrieve their drinks. Sweat rolls down her arms and face but she doesn't care, doesn't care about the stares and the other kids dancing with their backs to her. She basks in the rapidly moving lights and rolling white clouds generated from the DJ's fog machine.

Another fast tempo song ends and a ballad starts to play. Samantha frantically scans the room for Andrew, spots him by the drink table, trying to catch his eye so that she can lean her head on his shoulder and forget about the world for a few minutes.

Samantha sees him in what looks like a heated argument with a couple of his friends from the track team. They laugh and point in her direction. She knows that they are talking about her, but she tries to ignore them and get Andrew's attention.

She sees him throw the dark contents of a plastic cup in his friend Sean's face. Sean gives him a shove and Andrew marches away from the table towards her.

When he approaches, Samantha grabs him by the arm, tells him not to let Sean ruin their good time, tells Andrew that only the two of them matter tonight, that this moment is all that matters. Samantha spies the other couples, arms draped around their dates' necks, stealing kisses as the chaperones turn the other direction.

Andrew hesitates, his face scrunched up, the rage apparent in the creases of his forehead, but Samantha pulls the sleeve of his sports coat toward the dance floor.

They start to slow dance, their hands on each other's hips, bodies apart. Samantha slides her arms around his back and moves closer towards his chest, but Andrew's arms stiffen. After a few seconds, Samantha leans in again, but he pushes her away.

Avoiding each other's gaze, Samantha and Andrew rock from side-to-side, bodies barely touching, as the song plays.

Before the song ends, Andrew rips himself from Samantha and storms outside, the gym door clanging as he leaves.

Laughter and snorts from her classmates mingle with the final notes of the ballad; greens and blues wash over Samantha's face as she stands alone on the edge of the dance floor.

Holding back tears, not wanting her mascara to run down her face in black streaks, she crosses the dance floor, her heels clacking on the hardwood, pushing past some dangling streamers. She bursts out the door into the spring air.

Aside from a couple of kids sneaking cigarettes in the shadows of the gym parking lot, Samantha and Andrew are alone. He wraps his arms tightly around himself as if he'll fall to pieces if he lets go. Samantha tries to tell him that it's all right, they don't have to stay at the dance, that they can go to the diner down the street and get milkshakes, or they can just drive around with the windows down and sing along to their favorite songs at the top of their lungs, anything so long as they're together.

She places her palm on his back, and he flinches as if her touch burns. He twists around to face her and tells her that he's done here, time to go home, that the whole night was a dumb idea, to just forget it.

Samantha whispers a faint *okay* and follows him to the car. They drive through a night not yet fully dark with the radio on, but no one sings along to the music. Andrew's eyes fixate on the road.

He pulls up in front of her home and slams on the brakes, thrusting Samantha's body forward. She touches his arm; he doesn't flinch, but he doesn't turn towards her. He doesn't reciprocate her touch.

She wants to tell him so many things, to tell him to forget this night and the haters at school, that maybe in the morning everything will be better, that things will be the way that they were before.

But she doesn't say any of this. She mutters a fragile *text me* and exits the car. Andrew doesn't turn his head. Before she reaches her front door, Andrew peels out, the cacophony of distorted guitars and hardcore screams pulse in the air. Samantha watches Andrew barrel down the street as the red glow from his taillights fade away.

She opens her front door slowly. She sees her mother on the living room couch, eating potato chips watching a reality television show. Her mother doesn't say a word, just glances at Samantha and then continues to watch the television. Her father's car wasn't in the driveway, so he's probably not home yet, still boozing it up with his friends.

Samantha starts to cry now, to hell with her mascara. She takes off her high heels, grabs them by the straps and races upstairs to her room, slamming the door.

She looks in the mirror, her eyes puffy and black. She pulls her blue wig off. She stares at the short, black hair that she's been trying to grow out and runs her hand through it. She tosses her wig into her aluminum wastebasket and shoves a bunch of notebook paper on top. She rifles through her desk drawers and finds an old book of matches. She strikes a few matches and flings them into the wastebasket.

The hair and paper ignite into a flaming torch. The bra is the next to go. Then her heels. She watches them burn for a couple of minutes. She won't need them again.

Sam trundles through his two-story colonial, wine glass in hand, brimming with Chardonnay. A glass that has been filled and refilled.

His wife of four years, Nicole, is away on yet another business trip. She seems always to find an excuse to be away.

He wanders down the hallway past bedrooms devoid of children, rooms silent and dark. The silence carries an almost unbearable weight.

Sam stumbles towards his bedroom. He approaches his closet, stomach churning as if a tuna were flopping around inside of him. He puts the glass on a dresser, enters the open closet, and stretches his arms upward to reach an old shoebox on the top shelf. He sits on the ground with the familiar box, opening the lid. Inside is the charred blue wig that he wore years ago. When, for a brief moment, he called himself Samantha. Called himself by the name he should've been born with.

Sam runs his fingers through the singed, synthetic hair and entertains the thought of putting it on. Fuzzy images of Andrew appear in his mind. Tears begin to well.

He slams the lid on the box and shoves it back in its hiding spot. Sam rises and takes a large swallow of wine, then collapses on the bed and stares at the slow-moving blades from his ceiling fan, wishing for sleep—to dream of a better life, to dream of a life unlived.

THE CLASS OF 2000

ROBERT DEAN

When I got up this morning, murdering Alex Stanchon was *not* on my To Do list.

There isn't any blood, but Alex is totally dead—like, dead as a doornail dead. His eyes are open, but there's no one home. Dressed in his best track pants, and shirt reading *Deplorable Infidel,* he's stiff as a board. I think he might have voided his bowels because I'm noticing a stink.

I hadn't thought about Alex in forever. He was a machismo male monkey asshole who peaked senior year of high school. Last I heard, he sold paint in bulk to contractors.

We grew up in a working class suburb of Chicago. Coming up, we had two choices: make it out as an athlete or you're a trades guy. I knew like, four people who went to college. We played baseball. While Alex was above average, I cruised past him. His best shot at getting out of here was a state school or a community college with a good ball program.

Me, on the other hand, I was scouted by the major league clubs by my junior year. I had a nasty slider, an over-arching, Barry Zito curve, and a fastball straight from Hell. By the time I was seventeen, I was hitting the high nineties *and* I was lefty.

Scouts salivated over my two-seamer and cutter. They'd come by for chitchat, ask how my arm felt, or talk about my windup mechanics. Before I knew it, Cleveland scooped me up and signed me to a tiered performance deal. Alex hated my guts. He was used to being fawned over because he was a good-looking kid from whom everyone expected great things. Me? Forget it.

Despite my abilities on the mound, I didn't want that life of everyone wanting to be my BFF. I wasn't cool because I was a weirdo loner, it was because one of the worst kept secrets of our high school's sports program: I was gay. Am gay.

In 2000, coming out was still a huge deal. The closet was firmly in place, and every time something came up, I had to deny, deny, deny—despite having a boyfriend.

Alex knew about my secret. He tried to use it against me constantly. But as high school coaches with winning records are known to do—it was swept under the rug. So it goes in high school sports.

But to Alex and his knuckle dragging crew, I wasn't Devin or even Atienza, I was *Faggot*. Seriously. Faggot. That was my name. Despite being teammates, he refused to call me anything but. I dealt with it. I was okay. This wasn't the first time hearing a slur—you come out a gay man and you're bound to hear plenty on a daily basis, 'cuz these boys around here ain't wearing a San Francisco smile, they're in dirty Carhartt jackets and smell like Marlboro Reds.

My boyfriend was this tragic, beautiful boy named Apollo. He was perfect, like a little slice of cake. Apollo could paint, run track, and had mocha colored skin you could drink like a cup of dark roast. Apollo was out. He didn't give a single fuck what anyone thought, and he worked it. I was in awe of his bravery. Despite his initial reservations, he agreed I needed to stay out of the social spotlight. He showed way more adult-like thinking in spite of our ages than I ever could. He was headed for Manhattan's fashion district as soon as we graduated.

But those dreams of couture didn't stop him getting his ass kicked daily by boys who caught him in their bathroom or when he was just looking for a quiet place at lunch. His life was a constant carnival of misery. After a while, he started going to the bathroom at the nurse's station because it was easier.

And Alex was one of the goons tormenting. Once, he kicked him in the ass with a cleat, leaving a waffle print of social status defined through knuckle-dragging entitlement. I cringed at the thought of what Apollo went through. We'd lie in one another's arms after school and he'd show me his bumps and bruises, he didn't mind when I kissed them better.

I remember him crying when those kids were unbearably mean, cornering him in darkened hallways, asking him if he wanted to *suck their dicks*, or finding cruel ways to extend torture like scribbling *fairy* or *homo* on his locker. Because of my skills, I was moved along with a sense of *nothing to see here*, despite seeing everything once the halls were quiet.

I'd made it up through the ranks of Cleveland's minor league system. Within two years, I was their number one, straight up dealing in Columbus, their Triple-A affiliate. Cleveland signed me to a team friendly deal that netted me tall money with the promise that next go around, I was gonna make millions.

That next spring training, I hit camp and was on the Major League roster as their #5 starter. I consistently broke the high nineties, and even a hundred a few times. I was a legit fireballer. Hype around me was insane. But then, a game against Kansas City happened around July. I took a line drive straight to my right knee—the knee any lefty needs to pull their power from when they wind up. I went down immediately. We tried surgery, rehab, all of it. It was never the same.

I drifted around the league as a pitching specialist; I did camps, but never could command a secondary career. I was a rookie who went out on a lot of hype and half a season of play. I didn't have equity amongst Cleveland fans, just a *what could'a been.*

When the job opened up to be the head coach for my high school team, I took it. I'm not a flashy guy, so most of that MLB cash is in the bank. Taking the job with my school was about loyalty to the program that groomed me.

Being back around here was a swirl of emotions. Sure, when you visit your parents, or see old friends, it's ok. Because you're back to *your* home after a few days. But I moved back here, blocks from where I grew up. This place is like a living museum.

Driving around town, seeing things I'd buried, I'm incepting memories differently. I think about my time with Apollo. I don't pine for the past, but remember him fondly. Home feels like a lot of things, but for me, it was discovering my true self. Today, I'm out with my sexuality, but then? Whoa. It was a heavy topic.

I posted up in Mary's Tavern, a joint just down the blocks from my mom's place. I shot the breeze with Gillian, whom I knew from back in the day, too. I got caught up in the local gossip while she poured a stiff whiskey in return for my interested ear.

Things were going on just dandy until Alex strolled in with his crew of acolytes, still treating him like he was God. They headed for the pool table. It wasn't until he saddled up to the bar, about thirty pounds heavier than I saw him last, that he instantly recognized me.

"Faggot! Holy shit. What are you doing here?" He took a drink from his Bud, never breaking eye contact.

"It's Devin. I'm back in town. I'm the coach at the high school. Baseball, obviously."

"Heard about you losing your spot. Rough shit. Well, you're back with us assholes now. Still no fag bar in town, though. You'll have to head to the north side for that." He said just as he walked off to his crew. Within moments, I heard the snickers and saw stares from his cronies. Their leering eyes canvasing me, wondering about what I do in locked bedrooms that made my being, from my toes to my heart, feel covered in slime. Fuck this. After another Jameson, I got my steel up. I slid off my stool and walked over.

"Hey man, can I clear the air with you?" He looked at me like I was an incredulous asshole to waste his time about something happening so long ago.

"What's on your mind, bub." He crossed his arms.

"Uh, I was thinking about buying you a drink and talking like adults, not have a public forum."

"Say whatever it is you've got to say, dude. We're all men here," he paused, "well, *we* are."

I stood at the edge of the pool table, subconsciously running the tips of my left fingers along the green felt.

"Just wanted to say that all of the shit you talked was fucked up. I knew that you guys used to kick the shit out of Apollo. That was wrong. He didn't deserve that. He was kind. You acted like a cunt. I'd say you evolved, but obviously, nothing's changed."

"See, this is what's wrong with America. I can't have a fucking opinion. I hate fucking queers. I don't like black people. I stay away from them, and Mexican's too. I'm allowed my opinion, faggot." He crossed his arms, acting as a statement of finality.

I don't know why. But, something went black. Something feral inside of me, something located deep within my reptilian brain.

I thought of every image of rights stripped away, a protester spit on, or people standing in front of my flag, the rainbow flag. I thought about every slur I've had to shrug off, how I had to pretend I wasn't queer, how I had to sell myself out. I thought about Apollo and our innocent love. That love only comes once in your life, and it was tainted by cultural discordance. I felt sick.

Without ever registering my movements, the weight of the cue ball was like a bomb in my grip. Within seconds, the ball went from performing its functionary role, to hurling through the air and crashing into Alex's right cheek. The ball came of out of hand with wicked speed. I threw a perfect strike straight at Alex's face, and this time, I was the one who never broke eye contact.

The collision of skull mixed with the ball's hardness, given the close proximity, and the sheer force of an upper nineties speed register, dropped him. He never had time to react. I hurt my knee, not my pitching arm.

The sound of the ball crushing his skull wasn't unlike squeezing a drained pop can in a strong grip. People in the bar started screaming. I walked to my seat and went back to work on my drink. Despite recognizing the faces of this town a little worse for wear, I ain't about to let another person call me *faggot* ever again.

The sirens grow louder and Alex ain't coming back—he ain't going nowhere but the morgue. He's gonna be a chalk outline on the floor and the crux of a lot of urban legends passed down in this fucking town. Should'a known I throw strikes.

Play ball.

LEARNING TO LOVE

JENNIFER WILLIAMS

I have been in love exactly forty-five times. It's a lot, I know, but I fall in love so easily. A simple look, a soft whisper, or the gentlest of touches: all of these things can make me love you. And when I do, when like turns from a polite distance to the closeness of lovers, that's when things go bad.

My love leaves marks; it is like the rough blade of a knife in need of sharpening. Scars form that wind and twist like knotted rope, pink and red and white along your skin. It hurts when you touch it, and yet, you can't help but run your fingers along them, feeling their thickness and following their path like a maze written on your body. They are maps of our knowing, a guidebook on how not to be. But they are also like the touching of stars. Burning and bright and in the moments before being consumed, you are smiling and filled with childish glee.

The first time I fell in love was with a boy in school. He liked comic books and music, and when we kissed he would come and then blush and bow his head, ashamed of his quickness. His scars were the deepest because I loved him the most.

The next was with a girl I met at the beach. We snuck off to the trees that lined the sand and she let me touch her all over with my hands. She was warm and soft and she only cried a little when the first scars blossomed on her bronze hued skin.

The radio DJ played rock in the middle of the night and I would call him when I couldn't sleep. I'd ask him to play something quiet, classical or ambient or new age, and he'd do it every time. My love for him reached out like tendrils slipping along those air waves, a direct line to him. I heard he's married now. I wonder if she loves him because of his scars or in spite of them.

There is power in love. Like the time I loved the man who touched me when I said no. I loved him so hard that I scarred his heart, made it stop just long enough for me to escape. He is on a waitlist now. He spends his days in bed feeling bitter and victimized. He doesn't understand that his heart was poisoned all along.

I tried, earnestly, to love without leaving marks. There was the man in the grocery store who gave me a ride home. The girl at the art show who complimented my necklace. The neighbor who lent me a cup of sugar when I ran out. They were good people, I think. But they were kind and kindness has a price.

I lived on my own for a while, away from people, traveling from city to city on my bike. I'd watch the birds and the squirrels, sit on a wall by the ocean, or go for a walk in the woods, sometimes camping there. Those times were nice. I could love a flower without watching it wilt or a cloud in the sky without seeing it break apart and drifting away. But something would always bring me back to humanity and there'd always be another person to love.

Then, for a time, I embraced it. Skin was a canvas, I decided. I painted with abandon. I left so many bodies in my wake; young and old, man and woman. I felt alive, at first. So very vibrant and alive, intoxicated by first touches, by their smell and the sounds they made as we came together. But soon those unions became blurred. I lost sight of the place between pleasure and suffering. My love reached out, razor sharp, a vampire's tooth and claw ready to strike, desperate to be fed.

Everything I touched became scar tissue.

So I retreated, again, away from the world, to a place of solitude. But it's lonely. The nights seem darker somehow, and the days dull without the company of others.

They say if you really want to find love that you need to love yourself first. That's what I'm doing now, here in the confines of this tiny home by the sea.

It was slow, at first; an ungraceful climb out of a shallow grave. Here and there I would see the finest of white lines, the kind you get from a quick slice of glass when taking the trash out or doing the dishes. Nothing remarkable. Nothing too painful.

But I'm getting better. There's a scar on my inner thigh now, long and jagged, its color the bright red of a beating heart. I can feel the tattoo of my pulse in it, cracking like thunder as I learn to love myself.

They say love hurts.

It's true. It hurts like hell.

BROTHERS

LEO X. ROBERTSON

"And now you've forgotten," Bobby said, playing lazily with Sam's hair. They lay next to each other in Sam's bed, their naked skin glowing yellow with strips of streetlight that came through the window.

Sam took a lighter from the nightstand and lit the joint held between his lips. He took a puff and grinned. "Go on, then, what is it?"

Bobby took the joint from Sam's mouth and said, "Watch this." He took a puff and exhaled a jet of ethereal green cinders, which lit Sam's bedroom before they disappeared.

"H-How'd you do that?" Sam said.

"It doesn't bring back memories?" Bobby said.

"Of what? I've never seen anything like that before." Sam stroked Bobby's chest.

Bobby put the joint in a bedside ashtray. "Didn't think so."

"You're not gonna tell me how you did that?"

Bobby grinned and pulled Sam in, kissing his forehead. Sam laughed, but as he propped himself up on a pillow, he saw tears running down Bobby's face.

"Tell me how we first got together," Bobby said.

"You're so needy," Sam said.

"Last time," Bobby said. "I promise."

Sam got up and took his bathrobe from off the floor, tied its rope around his waist, and stood in front of the bed, preparing to give a performance. "One day, about ten years ago, you invited me to the park after school—which was weird, because you seemed to hate me at the time," he began. He stopped and looked at the ceiling. "So why did I agree to meet you there? Anyway, we..." His eyes glazed over. "I, um ... Fuck. That's it. I don't remember the rest." He chuckled nervously.

Bobby sat up and wiped his tears away. "So long as I'm alive, you never will."

"I'm high," Sam said, "and it's late. That's all." He returned to bed, climbing over Bobby on the covers and kissing him again. "Unless you're casting spells on me now?"

"Something like that," Bobby said.

"Whatever you're doing," Sam said, leaning in, "it works for me."

"Good," Bobby said.

Sam pressed his head against Bobby's chest, and was soon asleep.

"I just hope you forget about me too one day," Bobby whispered. "You're sleeping with a ghost and you don't even know it."

He snuffed out the joint's embers.

Dear Maeve,

I was so sorry to hear that Bruce passed away, and I'm sorrier still that it's taken me months to write to you—though I've spoken to so many people who told me you'd appreciate me getting in touch at all. I believe it. But I'm no less sorry.

Also—I mention this only because I haven't seen you in such a while—there was a reason I was so awkward when I saw you at Martha's funeral. She'd told me, several times no less, that she was waiting for you to call her after she'd gotten diagnosed. One of your fellow teachers from Hyndland even popped round once to tell Martha to just forget about you and not worry about it. I didn't agree, if that makes a difference.

I saw in your eyes at her funeral that you knew I was blocking you out emotionally. When you told me you hadn't even known she was ill, I froze. At the time, I didn't know that you didn't know.

But I don't write you to appease myself. I just wanted to say: I hope you're okay.

You and your family are in my thoughts.

Sam.

PS. How is Bobby doing? I guess I have no right to ask that either.

He'd written this on a tasteful card of rough, recycled paper with dried rose petals pressed within its folds. She stroked its furry edges and thought he'd made it especially for her—possibly in some class to alleviate depression through crafts.

She called him on the number he'd included, telling him that she did indeed appreciate that he'd gotten in touch and yes, since he brought it up, he had seemed distant at his mother's funeral. But that wasn't the reason she'd called. She had bad news about Bobby that was better delivered in person.

When Sam heard those words, he remembered the voicemail his father had left him more than five years ago: *It's not good news, son. Your mother's very ill. Come round as soon as you can, and pick up some tomato soup on the way.*

Maeve and Sam agreed to meet that Saturday at a favourite Queen Street café. She looked more stunning than he recalled: dark tan, feline eyes, sleek black hair. Her smile at the sight of him radiated a decade-old pang of guilt. The last time they were both here, he was seventeen, and she'd paid for lunch for him and Martha. He hadn't managed to finish his club sandwich and Maeve had teased him about it—affectionately, though that never computed with him.

They hugged, and he offered to buy her another coffee. She couldn't stomach it, but accepted anyway. After collecting their cappuccinos, he paced his way across the mosaic tiles, breathing in the room's rich vapour of roasted beans and pastries.

"You're looking well," she said as he returned to their table.

"Y-You wanted to tell me something about Bobby."

She stifled a laugh. "You were never great at small talk." She lifted the coffee and motioned for Sam to do the same. They sucked away the foam fern leaves from on top. "He's dead, Sam."

"What?"

"He got involved with the wrong people in Barlinnie." She caught a glance of herself in the steamy strip of mirror that ran around the room and picked off a clump of mascara. "Remember those guys in the news? The ones that kidnapped men from Byres Road and," she laughed, "raped them with screwdrivers? Sorry. Of course it's not funny." Her eyes followed the coils of green waves that curled around the floor. "Just never thought I'd end up saying something like that."

"God, I'm so sorry," Sam said.

"Yeah," she said, picking at her nails. "You're very sorry."

Without realizing, he stroked her hand. "I can't tell you how badly I wanted to go see him when he last got out. But I didn't know how to explain it to my boyfriend at the time." *Sorry, gotta go, my first love's getting out of prison.* He laughed too. "I didn't know if Bobby'd even want to see me."

"Of course he would have," she said. "He talked about you all the time. He was hurt that you stopped visiting—at first— but once he heard you were with someone new, he understood. He wasn't worth waiting for. You don't know what he was like when he got out. Whatever you'd done, it wouldn't have made a difference. Trust me on that or you'll drive yourself nuts."

As she picked her cup up again, he became distracted by the rustling of rolled paper that jutted from the pocket of her blazer. She saw him notice it and held it towards him.

"I don't know why I thought to give this to you," she said.

"What is it?"

Her head wobbled back and forth in thought. "When you got in touch, I remembered those years when Bobby hogged the family computer at night to chat with you online. I wondered if any of those conversations were saved." His eyelids flared in horror. "*I* wasn't going to read them, but I thought you might want to. Anyway, there was nothing on there but games, some silly holiday pictures, and this. It's a diary he kept when he was looking after Kevin. There's nothing about you in there, though. And it doesn't make for pleasant reading either."

"But it would be so good to... to hear from him again somehow," he said.

She nodded, and a swell of warmth passed between them.

The folded paper went into his jacket pocket.

Sam got back to his flat on the east side around dinnertime, still steeped in deathly ruminations. He took a shower, put on some-ex-or-other's old t-shirt, a cardigan and jeans, and set about preparing a single serving of Spaghetti Bolognese, eschewing his usual Monday practice of freezing and storing enough for the week. He stood leaning over his electric hob as the pot of spaghetti boiled, the vapor clouding over his face, and he tapped his feet to the syncopated beat of Coltrane playing from his laptop, echoing off the glass of his dining room table.

Bobby's diary lay unfurled, though curling, a little paper boat floating on the table's still sea, a spectre at his banquet for one. Sam looked at it and realized he was listening to music of the dead.

The world outside held the same dark blue sky of the evening he'd first invited Bobby over. They'd endured a few minutes of stilted small talk before pouncing on one another. When the weekend ended, Sam went back to work at a travel agency in town and Bobby went out and got himself arrested again. This became a tradition each time Bobby got out, irrespective of Sam's relationship status at the time, until he finally realized Bobby was never going to be his. Two lapses in judgement after that and he had to cut Bobby out his life entirely.

Finished the bottle of Chianti he'd told himself was just to flavor the sauce, Sam picked up the diary, retrieved his reading glasses from between two tall candles on the shelf behind him, and delved into the past.

Bobby

I looked into the smoky portal of Kev's room. It smelled like burning anti-flea collars. Mum had taken the door off its hinges. He sat at his PC, the monitor of it sitting at a strange angle on the old warped oak table he'd found in a skip last year. I walked to him with a sleeve covering my mouth and he jerked back when I placed a hand on his shoulder.

"Fuck," he said. "You can't do that to me when I'm reading about this shit."

Chemtrails, Illuminati, government hoaxes—the standard fare.

"Come sit with me a minute, Kev," I said.

"You wanna toke?"

He passed me the joint he'd had gripped between index and middle fingers and I took one hit. He didn't notice that I was paralysed on the floor, searing holes into his sheepskin rug, until he was antsy enough for his next draw. I developed a full-blown panic attack, my heart like boom-boom, boom-boom. He snatched the joint back from me and shot me an irritated look as if it was my fault we didn't get to talk that day.

"I'm thinking about strangling that mother behind you," he said.

I'd told mum what he was up to and she'd taken him to the doctor. They said it was skunk-induced psychosis and they didn't know what to do. Mum played too heavily on what great pals we were, tried to get *me* to be his mum, it seemed. Every day my heart would drop if I couldn't see his head poking out from the ball of sheets on his bed straight away, and I'd think, *that's it, he did himself in while we were asleep.*

Today, Mum had woken me up and presented Kev to me at my door like he was some nervous little primary school kid and then said, "Your brother had the wonderful idea of taking you out to McDonald's with his allowance. You like McDonald's, don't you, Bobby?"

Kev had looked like he'd be crushed if I'd said no, so I'd walked him here, made sure he'd gotten some sunlight, and here we sat in front of each other.

I thought meeting his eye would be seen as aggressive, so I let him sit silently in my company as if everything was fine. He nibbled on his McChicken Sandwich to make it last as long as possible. I stuffed my gub with my salad because he kept saying unanswerable, depressing things like, "I'm trying really hard not to slam my head into the window right now."

Some of these things I thought he might do and others appeared just melodrama. But who was I to tell them apart?

"You're not trying, Kev," I said. "You're succeeding."

We got home and I told Mum Kev was unstable. She said it would be fine for me to miss some classes to make sure he was okay. I disagreed.

"Don't you care about your mother at all?" she said.

"About Kev, you mean. Of course I do, but I'm not equipped to deal with him by myself. I'm not a nurse and I'm barely passing at school as it is. Can't you bring someone in?"

"Stop feeling sorry for yourself and do this, would you?"

We rephrased this central argument to each other several times. I kept losing.

I bathed Kev, fed him three times a day. I was with him every waking hour. A growing stack of orange-enveloped letters from the school poked out the rubbish, but we couldn't trust that if I so much as looked away from him, he wouldn't jump out the window or stab himself in the neck. Too often his gaze sought the nearest destructive implement, eyelids flaring when nail scissors, secateurs, or letter openers called back to him, glinting.

When I told Mum I was mentally prepared for the day it happened she said, "You can't say that."

"Why not?"

"We don't say those kinds of things in this family."

Kev and I slept in the same bed, side by side. I think we both got—how would I put it?—too accustomed to the closeness.

When the school mentioned a trip to India, Mum suggested I could go, her way of telling me she knew the arrangement between Kev and me wasn't cool.

I started reclaiming increments of my own time to get Kev used to the idea that I'd be gone for a full week. He sobbed all hours of the day and had several therapy sessions to get him convinced he was ready to see me go, but his brain was shot to shit. He couldn't learn anything, couldn't grow anymore, a damaged little boy who only got worse, and seeing this, Mum soon inverted India into a display of my blatant disregard for Family, forgetting, or making herself forget, that it was her idea for me to go.

She told Kev it would be a nice conciliatory gesture if he drove me to the airport. This was a real test of what we would leave unsaid. Would she really let one child wrap the other around a tree before admitting the dynamic she'd established wasn't working?

I couldn't sleep the night prior to the flight. A whole hour before my alarm was set, I got this weird feeling in my stomach. I ran across our soaking patio, twigs digging into my bare feet as I hobbled over to the garage, and I yanked up the door to find Kev running the engine of Mum's sedan.

A note glued to the window said: *You did this.*

Had to mean me, had to know...

I pulled the driver-side door open and dragged him out onto the driveway, slapping him about and saying "How fucking dare you!"

He wailed and flailed, just as angry at me for making him live. I lay beside him on the wet brick and the dense spring air cooled us.

Needless to say, I guess, I didn't go to India.

I couldn't look at Kev for a week. I even moved back into my own room and all of us got driven spare by his night-howls. They penetrated right through the foam earplugs that I soon had piled up in small pyramids in the corners of my cabin bed.

After a month, he stopped. I got up in the night to check that he was still alive and found him sitting up, dressed and reading by himself. I apologized for interrupting him and even bowed as I left the room.

The morning after, around a breakfast bar of toast, eggs, marmalade, coffee, he offered to get in the shopping for us, with an overly enthusiastic ready-to-enter-the-world-again expression on his face. Mum and I said, "Wow!" at the same time in the same condescending tone, and we stood by the door as he left, waving to him proudly.

I sat playing the N64 in my room when Mum burst in and said, "It's Kev." She was on the phone. "He's about to get on the underground. Uh huh? Okay, son. Yep. I love you too. We all do. Always have, always will." She hung up.

Know how she broke the news? She said, "He made the choice." The fuck did that mean?

I pushed past her and ran down the stairs, tripping as I skidded round the landing and fell down the bigger flight. Mum caught up to me, curled foetally in the foyer, but as her consolatory hand touched my arm I scrambled up and ran into the kitchen, screaming in some nonsense language as I pulled down on the row of plastic cabinets, tugging them off their brackets. China cups and plates spilled to the floor. I picked up shards and smashed them against the stony tiles before collapsing onto the white, ruinous heap.

I got this feeling, an angel of relief rising from my body.

Sam read the last lines while lying down on his mother's expensive and solidly stuffed leather couch, tears running from the corners of his eyes. Wine duly drained, his first idea was to pick up his phone and call Hugo.

"Yeah?" said a voice on the other end in a parched morning bark.

"Bro," Sam said, coughing out sobs. "You're still alive."

"Duh," Hugo said. "You just woke me up. What the hell time is it in Glasgow? What are you doing with yourself?"

"I don't know, I just—"

"What's up?"

"I saw Maeve today."

"Mum's friend? Why?"

"I sent her a card about her husband passing away and she invited me out for a coffee."

There was quiet at Hugo's end. "Here," he said finally, "I've got to go to work soon, but it would be easier if we chatted on Skype."

Sam moved into the bedroom. The late-hour darkness, amplified by the thick curtains that excluded all but a narrow wavy band of streetlight that ran along the ceiling, set the mood for his reflections. Soon, Hugo called on Skype. Sam pressed the green phone button, and a tired chap who shared his mother's hazel eyes appeared.

"How's it going, bro?" Sam said.

"I want to say sorry for how I treated you when we were growing up."

Sam frowned and cranked his head back, catching a glimpse of his double chin in a glass frame before him, which held a colorful oil painting of a woman upside down in a sunny field. Sam's father bought it as it reminded him of Martha and gifted it to Sam when he decided he could no longer look at it. "Where is this coming from?"

"It's just something I've been thinking about for a long time, and we haven't talked. What's going on with you, bro?"

Hugo's curiosity was enough to make Sam cry. "Maeve gave me some diary Bobby kept about Kev."

"Kev, huh?" Hugo said. He looked at the empty wine glass in Sam's room. "That's not the best material to read when you're drinking."

"It reminded me that, like you say, you go over these old memories you resent about when we lived in the same country, and I forget that you're still out there, trying to do better. I've thought so badly of you. Sorry."

"We've all done things we regret, Sam. Jesus! You sure like to beat yourself up."

"If I'd just stopped taking offence at every turn and tried to understand how you were hurting, maybe... maybe you wouldn't have left and you'd be living here with me and our friendship would be so much stronger."

"You're forgetting how insufferable I was," Hugo said. "I'm gonna send you something, and you're gonna promise me that you don't show it to anyone else. It's my diary, from when I was seventeen."

"Wait, is this *the* diary? The purple ring-binder one with the toucan on the front?"

"The one and only," Hugo said, laughing.

Sam doubled over in pain. How long would it take for the diary to reach Glasgow?

He heard a *blip* and looked to see *Diary.PDF* attached to the conversation.

"I destroyed the original," Hugo said. "But not before scanning it. Funny, I would've died if you'd read it back then, but now? I mean, I did those things, but I was someone else. It's just a dream I once had. I don't know why I thought to give it to you now, but I get the sense it's what you need. So if it's cool with you, I'm gonna try and fit in a run before work."

Sam had his arms folded on the desk. He nodded, looking away from the screen as his brother disappeared once more.

Hugo

Today I slept until the afternoon. I set an alarm so I could wake up, eat some brownies, and go back to sleep to make sure they kicked in by the time I got to work. Mum asked if she could drive me. I said it was fine. She said she had a list of things for me to do around the house when I got back. I said I wouldn't do those things. She scolded me for not paying rent, but looked defeated and invited me to Starbucks for a coffee and a chat about what I was doing with my life. She said she didn't know what was going on with me anymore. I was hardly the one to ask, even less so when the brownies kicked in while both of us were staring into our grande caramel lattes. I sat there in silence, thinking she knew. She looked sadder and sadder.

"I'm washing these plates with cream," I said to Chef.

"You're out your nut again, Hugo," he said.

I looked down at the creamy plates in the sink and there were waterfalls of blood down my forearms. I pulled my gloves off and screamed. Had I cut myself on the shards of plates, glass, and knives that the old biddy with the leathery arms always left at the sink's base?

Chef came over and asked what was up with my nose and I sneezed chunks of bloody septum on him.

"Aw for fuck's sake, Hugo. You can't be snorting coke at work. Go home." Chef was lenient: he'd told me he'd ruined his own brain with pills, that when his son was born, he knew it should've been the happiest day of his life but he felt nothing.

"Did I do bad?" I said.

"You've got to slow down."

I went to the bathroom. Tears ran over the blood that streamed from the delta of my nose. I thought it was blood. It was bright and red, but solid like wax. I peeled it off and washed my face.

It must have been after midnight when I left. I was walking down Buchanan Street, awash with the blue of the streetlights, taking in the scent of clean wet stone, when I bumped into that junkie who always says he'll stab me if I don't give him fifty p. I ignored him. A group of girls left the purple neon outline of some trashy club so I stopped them to talk. I asked the prettiest one if she wanted to go out for a drink with me sometime. Her friends laughed and they kept walking without giving me an answer.

When they walked away, a figure appeared behind them. A woman, naked, skin shining green. I first thought it was black hair streaming down her body, but I traced its river from her thighs back up to the source: her nose. It was dried blood.

Bobby, from the year below, invited me over to his house for a session. We sat outside, smoking green with his mum's glass bong from Amsterdam. What sun there was soon faded, so Bobby said we could go inside because his mum, Maeve, had pre-rolled some joints.

"Look at your boots!" Maeve said to me from the stairs when we stepped through the door. She was wearing a frumpy black dress and too much makeup. "You could kick somebody's head in with those boots. The frog is under the mulberry bush." She hugged and folded her arms, stamping her feet and pouting like a child. "I don't want to go."

"Mum's out of it," Bobby said to me. "Are you gonna go dressed like that?"

"Go where?"

"Kev's funeral."

All I remember about it was being terrified that people knew how high I was. I clung onto Bobby and he carted me around the buffet. He'd spent months caring for Kev and now here I was leaning on him. He said my eyes were red but not to worry because most of their family would have been out their nuts on drugs and that anyway.

"Why didn't you tell me?" I said.

"Tell you what?" Bobby said. "That Kev died? Fuck. I thought you knew. Were you guys close?"

"I don't know." I started crying again.

"Jesus, Hugo. I only invited you because—come out to the car with me for a second."

In his trunk were gym bags full of Monster spray paint and new double-filter masks for both of us.

"Wow," I said. "Must have been well dear."

"I didn't go to The Artstore," he said. It was a place we made fun of, where all the cans were marked up for spoiled School-of-Art twats' awful final-year installations. "There's this other place in Paisley where you can barter. It's a real shame. There's these kids that hang out there all the time, and the owner's constantly scolding them for nicking, as if they're all pals and that. It'll go under for sure. Hey, we could probably slip out now and go do some throw-ups at this place outside of town?"

He drove us to his site and I did some quick pieces in the poorly lit mouth of an underpass. There were these guys watching me. And I saw that woman again, the one from Buchanan Street. Why was she following me?

I ran to Bobby, all paranoid, and asked him if what we'd smoked was the same shit Kev died from. He asked why I thought that, and I pointed at the woman staring at me. She stood on bare concrete with like barbed wire and broken bits of wood all around her. Her skin looked green again, and the wet black hair over her breasts held fragments of cardboard.

"You can't see her?" I said.

"Hugo, you've been freaking out all day. Are you gonna drop to your knees to try and dig your way out of here too, the way you did at T in the Park?"

"I've always been a bad tripper. But on weed?"

"Why don't you go down by the tracks? There's some great walls there and it'll be dead quiet now."

I walked down a valley of dirt, my eyes fixed on the dull sheen of tracks. They were below me, then above me as I skipped down an incline, meeting a fox boxing a mouse in the cleft before I climbed back up the dirt and rubble.

A train passed. In the slim passage by the wall, beyond the tracks, I threw Bobby's gym bag down and took out some cans. I began to spray a seafoam H, but then I heard barking not far away. I was still tripping, surely. I looked around: moonlight ran across the metal tracks, broken by shadowy stalks of dandelions. Off in the distance, beyond Bobby's abandoned factory, monolithic cooling towers belched plumes of water that condensed in the cold air and rose up in orange light, occluding the hills beyond them.

I heard the echoes of stones hitting the train tunnel walls. The white teeth of a German Shepherd flew out the dark and its jaws opened and clamped down on my leg, the keen pressure of them against my bones instantly sobering me up. Two torches, held by policemen, flashed in my face.

British Transport Police, they were. When I arrived back home with them, Mum stood fuming by the door, wearing one of her long black shawls and her coloured bangles. Men stampeded about the house, opening the drawers, nicking all my cans.

"Bastards have got nothing better to do," I said when they left. "You see all these bruises their fucking attack dogs gave me? This is ridiculous."

"You promised me you'd stopped," Mum said.

"I do this because of you. The Paris trip, for my sixteenth? I saw all the cool graffiti there and it made me want to start. You inspired me."

"No matter what you saw when you were out getting high on Parisian park benches, here in Glasgow, you're scribbling your initials on all manner of road signs, garage doors, power boxes—"

"Mum, I'm gay."

"What the fuck?"

"So it's okay when Sam tells you he's gay but it isn't okay when I do it? Why can't you just accept us? I'm going to get a job in a gay place. I can't be a KP anymore."

"I... well, I'm glad you want to do something other than be a kitchen porter. That was never for you, son."

"Why do you always talk about it as if it was a career move for me? Your other son works in retail."

"He's gonna go to uni."

"You don't know that."

"Well, you're not going to uni and you're not paying rent so whatever you think you're doing with your life, it had better pay."

When I started working as a bartender at Parlour, Mum and Maeve sat by the bar to support me, watching me flip bottles to get tips. They said it seemed like a *nice, cool, respectable* place. It sure was, during the day.

That night, I jumped over the bar and pushed through the crowd to go out for a smoke, just to get away from it. Outside was further awash with partying riffraff from the adjacent *straight places*, as most of the other bartenders at Parlour called them. I couldn't breathe. I undid my belt a little as a group of lowlife neds walked by, swigging clear liquid from an Irn-Bru bottle. It was probably straight vodka.

"Got somethin' stuck up your arse there, gayboy?" one of them said.

"No," I said. "Wanna help me with that?"

"You bein' cheeky to me?" said one of their girlfriends, trotting across the lane's cobbles towards me in her clear heels.

I tried to say "Duh" in response, but before I could, she flung a fist out at me. I winced as I received her punch above my ear, which began to ring, and when I looked to the street again, she and her crew had gone.

Graham, one of the other new guys, came out the bar and asked me what happened. He seemed nice, so I let myself cry.

People were so fucking ungrateful though, never seemed to appreciate when others were vulnerable in front of them.

"Smile, mate," he said. "Why aren't you smiling?"

"I don't feel like smiling," I said.

"Getting any sex tonight?"

"What?"

"Bet I could put a smile on that dour face of yours."

"I don't want to have sex with you."

"Don't act like it's such a big fucking deal," he said, "like you've never fucked a stranger before. No! Haven't you? Never?"

"I've never been with anyone before."

"Then how the fuck can you call yourself gay?"

He returned to the bar. By the end of the night, he'd even gotten the customers involved in making sure I went home with him. Around closing time I realized they were helping me out, could see I needed company.

Poppers make your heart pump too quickly, make you feel like you're gonna faint. They don't make your arse feel loose at all.

When I got home, I woke up Sam to tell him about poppers because I thought he should probably know for later, since he was gay too. I told him to come to the kitchen with me for a cup of tea. I told him what was up with me recently—all the stuff I'd been trying out to feel whole, human—about the graffiti and the bar and the horrible things they said to me and made me do. I told him what I'd seen in the sex shop across the road from the bar, about the big black silicone fists and the nipple clamps.

"They fucking use that shit on each other, Sam," I said.

I told him how the British Transport Police had nothing better to do than make Mum upset. I told him that I loved him and asked if he loved me.

"Of course," he said.

I told him everything I would have wanted a big brother to tell me about the outside world and how it is. I was talking for so long that the sun came up and he had to go to school. I told him he was a great listener and that I wanted to talk to him again soon.

I woke up when I heard Sam's bedroom door slam shut from across the upstairs hallway. I thought maybe he'd had a bad day, so I opened his door and tried to cheer him up by showing him the pics of graffiti I'd saved on a USB. I told him that since he'd been at school, I'd gotten a text from Graham, who wanted to meet up that evening. I asked Sam if he was happy I had a boyfriend. He said, "Sure," but he still looked pissed off. I didn't know how to ask what was up. Sometimes when I opened his door I saw him writing in a journal, which he always snapped shut and hid in the drawer of his desk. I made a note to read it when he wasn't home, because all I could think to do was show him more pics. All he said was, "Hmm," so I came out with it.

"What's up, Sam?"

"I don't want to condone what you do."

"Look at these fucking buildings. They're in the middle of nowhere. I make them brighter. There were just plain concrete walls before I came in and painted them. Fuck's your problem?"

Graham wanted me to meet him back at the bar. He'd bought me a beer. The other guys watched us, proud of what they'd done.

"Listen," Graham said. "Last night was fun, but I've since found someone else."

"Hey, fuck you," I said. "You're the one who made me think you wanted to see me again. I didn't care."

"You're making a scene."

The other guys were laughing. I downed the beer and ran out and got back in Mum's S-Class. I drove to an offie and bought a bottle of Glen's. I sat in the car and drank and kept crying.

Guys are just the same as girls. I'd need to tell Sam to stay away from them in case the reason he said he liked guys was because he thought he could stick with them to prevent the pain.

I drove to Blythswood Square, where a few girls tried to get my attention, but I said I wasn't interested.

I parked in a lane and passed out. When I woke up, someone was knocking on the window. She stood there in the lane's green light, wearing a skirt and a hooded orange raincoat. Her wet hair smelled of lavender and cardamom; I could see now that it was dark purple.

"You found me," I said.

"I think you found me, honey," she said. "It must be time."

"Can we do it here? In the lane?"

"I have a place."

I got out and we walked back the lane. Her jingling keys shone brightly as she walked by a cocktail bar and ducked into an alcove to open the door to her block of flats.

The room she stayed in was a flat unto itself, with a sink and bath over by the window and nothing but a cupboard or two for all her belongings.

She took off her clothes and gave me her prices.

"You're a witch, aren't you?" I asked, stripping down to my boxers.

"If tonight, you're my wizard," she said.

"I was being serious."

I nuzzled into her skin, green with the street's weird glow. I lay her down on the bed and got up to take a condom from the crumple of my jeans. I pulled off my boxers, wrapped up my dick, and climbed on top of her, slipping myself into her cunt. I felt the warm wet walls of it tight against me. I would come if I kept going, so I lay on her chest and kissed her tits and built the momentum of my thrusts. Not minutes later, with my eyes closed, with her nothing but a wet shadow on the bed, my head burst with golden fractals of pleasure and I screamed out, "Thank you, thank you!"

"I was what you needed," she said.

"I could swear you found me."

"You're not leaving now. Smoke this green with me. I'll add it to your tab, and when you're ready to go again, we're gonna do it bareback. I swear you'll want to pay extra, because it feels so much better."

We kept our clothes off. We smoked up using the bong she'd stored on the shelf above her single bed. Her sweat dried coolly on my skin.

"This time," she said, "you're going to fuck me up against the wall."

Too much vodka had reached my veins. I couldn't get hard, so I sat on the bed and wanked for a bit and she waited with her arms above her head, pressed up against the oily strip of wall by the door that had no appliance, furniture, or radiator. She blended into the darkness again, and like that, I knew she was ready for me.

When I was hard, I walked into the dark portal of the room's corner and found her, thrust my dick inside her. It did feel so much better, and with the joy this gave me, I felt good enough to lift her up and fuck her. She was screaming about how good it was and our skin was green and clear and together, like we were this one glass statue, frozen in that moment in time. I came so fucking hard my legs gave in and she collapsed on top of me. Her hair fell over my face and she laughed.

"Don't worry," she said. "That was amazing."

"I've never done that before."

"Are you sure? You seemed like a pro."

"I'm only seventeen."

"You look much older!"

"Thanks so much for tonight."

"Oh no," she said, pressing a hand to her stomach, "thank you."

Sam sat in his own dark portal, his head gently clearing of the alcohol's blur, mood blending with the night's dream. He scratched at his crotch, finding himself aroused. There was a time when he would have done anything to know the grim details of his brother's adventures out the house. The diary had read like some fantasy he himself had concocted to cure salacious needs. Did Hugo know he felt that way?

He took the laptop back through to the kitchen, setting it by the sink on the dark granite countertop, before pulling open his corner cupboards in search of alcohol reserves meant for guests. He found a half-empty liter of Russian Standard and poured a large measure of it over heavily frosted ice, stirring it with a teaspoon. A breath of condensation gathered on the outside of the glass. He brought it to his lips and tilted a small sip's worth into his mouth. It tasted of nothing but ice water: he marvelled at how far he'd come since his early gag-inducing gulps from room temperature bottles removed from hoody pockets. Almost all his learnings from the past ten years or so were hidden in these little unconscious habits, such that it didn't feel like he'd learned anything at all.

Frowning, he had a sudden thought, and returned to the bedroom, placing his glass down on a nearby bookshelf. Yes, it was the same desk from his teenage bedroom, but he'd never kept a journal, had he?

The others had, but...

From out the thin gap around its single drawer came a low, green light. He opened the drawer. Nothing but pens, a broken ruler, a roll of Sellotape. A divider at the back prevented it from extending any further, but the drawer was shallower than the width of the desk itself.

Maybe...

He crawled beneath the table and felt around the open back of the tray that pulled out from the frame, gasping as his fingers touched paper, a stack of it. Freed, he saw that it was old graph sheets, which fell over his hands like wet cloth. He read a date at the top of the first page. It was ten years ago. By the night's supernatural logic, he had achieved the right to read on.

Sam

Today, after school, I went with Mum to Bobby's house, so she and Maeve could catch up. I guess Hugo had better things to do. Not me. So I stood amidst the garden's hearty weeds eating a gamey chicken skewer over a paper plate while watching Bobby dance around the bonfire with a rolled-up sheet of newspaper that he'd lit and was holding like a torch. He *toked* on it and laughed hysterically.

Mum and Maeve sat on the veranda, surrounded by citronella candles and empty bottles of wine. They were soon shouting at each other. A kid in one of Mum's English classes had recently killed himself and Maeve wasn't being supportive.

Mum shouted, "When you wanted to leave Sean, you turned up at *my* doorstep with your face all black and blue and *I* took you to file the divorce papers before you changed your mind, and *I* got Bobby and Kev out your house while you hid back at mine!"

The kid who'd killed himself was called Adam. Once, he'd been in an English class with a supply teacher and when Mum had asked him about the teacher, he'd said, "You want the pupil version, or my version?"

I heard this almost-anecdote countless times. Mum couldn't let go of the sliver of wit the kid had displayed. People are even duller dead than they are alive.

Bobby pulled out a quarter bottle of Glen's and spat a mouthful on the fire, which spewed green flames. I guided him into the toolshed at the end of the garden, trying to calm him down. He slumped between big rusty shears and a push mower, his head rolling about on the dirty wheel of a bike hung on the wall behind him. Woodlice skittered across the grimy, dust-flecked floor.

"Wanna give me a blowjob, poof?" he said.

"No."

"How come? I thought you fancied me."

I was silent.

"Know where my name comes from?" he said. "Bobby Sands. My dad gave me it. When I was a toddler, he used to sing to me." He drunkenly waved a finger through the air.

> Could you go a chicken supper, Bobby Sands?
> Could you go a chicken supper, Bobby Sands?
> Could you go a chicken supper
> Ya dirty fenian fucker
> Could you go a chicken supper, Bobby Sands?

Again, I failed to respond.

"Then the next verse goes: *Could you go a tin o' Coke tae wash it doon?*"

I had *She'll Be Comin' Round the Mountain* burling round my head the rest of the night. He took a swig of Glen's, stuffed the bottle down the front of his joggers and said, "Fuck you. That *is* funny."

That night, after waking up to piss, I had a wank while thinking about Bobby. He'd once beaten me and peed on me down the lane behind the refectory, but apparently that hadn't turned me off. When I was done, Mum got up from my couch. She'd come into my room in the night and fallen asleep there.

She said, "Your father snores," and left.

Later I woke up to Hugo rapping on my window. He must have scaled the drainpipe outside. I was so tired when I walked over to him that after bumping into a sharp corner of my desk, I asked him what he wanted.

"Whaddya think? Let me in!" he said.

I looked beyond him and saw that he'd parked Mum's car at a weird angle in the driveway, so that two of its wheels cut sad, muddy eyebrows out the garden's grass.

"What the fuck were you doing?" I said.

"Me and one of the chefs from my old work went to feed ducks some grapes down by the Clyde."

His eyes were big and black and I filled in the gaps.

"Hurry up, then." I opened the window and climbed back up the ladder to my bed, which he took as an invitation to join me, lying beside me and leaning his head against my chest like it was a mother's comforting bosom. He kept me up until four a.m. confessing all kinds of horrible things, telling me I had to ward off men if I had any sense, and everyone else if I had any interest in a happy life.

He later climbed back down, missing the ladder's last step and bashing his chin against one of the rungs. Sitting at my desk, he pulled out a USB drive and made me join him to look at his latest collection of vandalisms. He did this a lot, always under the pretence that I was his special little buddy. I was done protesting. He was going to keep coming back.

The next day our chemistry class visited the Glasgow Science Centre. After wandering around the exhibits by myself, I stood with my ear to the centre of a big radar dish. A group of kids waited by the other dish at the opposite end of the room. They were too far away for me to see who it was, but I recognized one of the voices.

"Suck my dick, gayboy," it said.

I turned to the dish and spoke into it. "Kill yourself, fenian."

A figure staggered away from the other dish. Surely I hadn't so easily managed to offend him?

When I followed his path, I found him leaning on a railing outside. It had been fairly warm in the museum, but Bobby's pits dripped wet strips the full length down his shirt on either side. He'd draped his blazer over the railing and folded his tie around a fist. I stood on the periphery of his personal space, sharing his view of the placid river, the skeletal bridge, the blocky BBC Scotland building.

"I win, pussy," I said.

He smiled. "I can't talk now. Meet me at Victoria Park. Main gate. Nine tonight."

"Why would I do that?"

A shiver ran across his shoulders. I wanted to reach out a consolatory hand, but the rest of our group quickly spilled out the building's front, and Mrs McCafferty barked in her angry man-voice at us to get on the Silver Fox bus. Bobby turned, put his blazer back on and pushed past me.

When I cycled up alongside Bobby at the unusually quiet double roundabout, his legs loosened. We were silent even after chaining our bikes to the railings. I watched him climb up the front gate, walking his way along a single railing, his Vans folding around its edges. Once he was over, he waited with his back to me. There was a snicker when I failed to find my footing a few times. Soon I was up and over too, but the point of a spike at the top of the gate poked itself into the flesh of my thigh enough to bruise.

We paced our way along the tree-shaded path.

"We're going this way," he said. "I wanna show you something."

"Wait. Before you take me any further, tell me why you asked me to meet you here."

"Fair enough," he said.

We walked by commemorative benches in one of the park's flower gardens, its misty air holding the clean metallic scent of marigolds, which grew on semi-circular soil slopes hidden by the night. He told me a long story about his brother Kev and we marched funereally beyond weeping willows to the semi-frozen lake with its roaming swans and ducks.

Over the flaking bridge, we found a green gate that locked off a small island. Barren branches and sad shrubs covered the space. Climbing on the bridge's side, we vaulted over the gate and walked through an accretion of dead wet leaves in which I spotted some condoms and what looked like trigonometry homework that had been folded into a point and used to wipe its owner's arse.

Bobby turned to look at me, his face wet with tears. He lurched forwards and his lips hit mine. We kissed. We pressed our foreheads together and closed our eyes.

Before I even had a moment to savour my first kiss, it was interrupted by a sobbing so surreal it sounded backwards, and way too loud for its source. There was a woman through the trees, by the pond. Her legs were spread open and she was up to her knees in scummy duck water, her dress hiked up far enough to reveal a child's crowning head like a big glossy eye. We clambered over the gate and ran to the woman, pulling her back from the water. Bobby took off his hoody and folded it beneath her.

"Push! Breathe!" we shouted at her, panicked, looking around and seeing nothing but useless, distant zombie-like couples.

"Don't look at me," she said in a new, gruff voice.

She groaned and pushed harder. Cupping my hands beneath her, soon the child spilled out onto the hoody, and I proceeded to wrap him. All the day's heat had risen into the night. Bobby kneeled behind the woman and propped her up. The wet asphalt soaked her dirty dress.

"What were you trying to do?" I said. "Kill him?"

She panted for a while, unable to say anything, tears rolling down her face, as she leaned back with exhaustion. When her breathing slowed, she said, "Look at him. He's already dead."

I turned away from the corpse; Bobby scooped it up in the hoody, its cord and veiny bag of afterbirth naturally following, glistening wetly in the moonlight.

"What a gift," he said.

I looked through my eyes remotely, my soul in some far-off location even less familiar, headed further still when she said to Bobby, "You're one too?"

"Yes," he replied, cradling the baby, shushing it. I kept expecting it to scream, but its skin was unpromisingly blue.

"Take him," she said. "He must have been meant for you."

"Sam, I have to go," he said.

Before I could reply, he ran off with the bundle held tight in his arms. I helped the woman up and she raked her fingers through her wet purple hair to clear away dead leaves.

"What just happened?" I said.

She turned around. The moonlight on the ragged curls of her hair swayed in the deep shadows. As I walked forwards, I saw that the shadow had become the wet asphalt, and the light on her hair was the weeping willows off in the distance. She'd disappeared and I was alone.

When I arrived home, I saw that every light but the bathroom's was out. On the partially lit landing. The jeans of someone sitting on the steps poked from the gloom. I crept up the stairs and found Mum's huddled figure pressed against the wall.

"Hung himself," she said.

"Hugo?"

"Adam. The kid from my class." Her face was a death mask. "They'd first told me it was pills, that he'd simply fallen asleep. But," she raised her hands as if directing her pupils on the theatre stage, "his parents left in the morning. It was a Saturday. They had no clue. He'd even asked his mum to get him a loaf of bread when she nipped down the shops. He made a loop of leather and hung it from his bedroom ceiling somehow. It would have been so painful, and he was alone. Sam, if I feel like this, imagine how his poor mother must feel!"

I recognized the scream that followed. It was borne from the need to purge all emotion, memory, love of the boy from herself at the expense of everything he ever gave her, and the prospect of the inevitably lengthy grief ahead so intimidating that she tried to do away with him in one excruciating burst.

After I got the confidence to ask Bobby what happened in the park, he said to meet him out at an abandoned factory building on the south side of town. It was a good half-hour walk from the nearest train station. I arrived at the factory mesmerised by the rushing of cars along the overpass, such that it became the sound of blood pulsing in my ears. Like decomposing bodies, the dead, discarded buildings released their gases.

I came back to life when a hand slammed down on my shoulder. Bobby kissed the back of my neck and guided me through one of the building's decaying apertures. Inside, a group of homeless men, ten at least, slumped against a wall and moaned wearily. After we scaled the yellow rungs stuck into a concrete beam at the back of the room, Bobby dashed away, which left me convinced once again that he was up to something.

Upstairs was pure darkness. In the distance, the scattering click of bouncing marbles echoed. Light sparked from grapefruit-sized baubles that he'd cast along the concrete.

Crouched up against the rear wall, he rolled the sleeves of his white t-shirt back and proceeded to struggle with a power cable, white clouds of his breath puffed into the room's fluorescent chill. He walked back towards me, swerving out the way of what I then saw was a large black metal spool, which he sat down on, pulling me closer, grinning as he kissed me. I brought my knees up onto the spool's edge, sitting in his lap, tugging his hair.

"I brought vodka," he said.

"Why?"

"Why did I bring it?"

"Why did you bring me?"

"I'll show you."

He sat me beside him and removed his trademark quarter bottle of Glen's from a satchel without breaking our kiss. He filled his mouth with vodka and lay me down on the spool's freezing surface. I looked up to nothing, into an infinite black, until the world returned in his touch. My lips followed the motion of his like we'd pressed our faces against a mirror. Vodka flooded my mouth, his fire flowed into me, and I swallowed it up.

I pushed his head back to look at him. "How did you find this place?"

He stood and tugged me behind him, his hand tight on my wrist. We reached the back wall where he'd been playing with the cable. There, a big industrial freezer hummed. A whited sepulchre of a thing that any number of creatures might have been sleeping in, I suspected. He took a key from his back pocket. My hand blocked the slot. He stabbed the key fiercely into my palm without seeing it.

"Shit!" he said. "What are you doing?"

"Bobby, before you show me what's in here, I want you to know, you can keep testing me but I'm not gonna leave you."

He snickered and tickled my palm so that I jerked it out the way. In slipped the key. He leaned the heels of his hands against the freezer's lid and pushed so the rubber lining unstuck. He half-dove into the freezer's empty maw and pulled out a ball of cloth. It was his hoody from the park, frozen.

"Is that...?" I took it from him and unwrapped it, unsticking the layers of cloth from each other to reveal a solid, doll-like baby with frost all over its skin, the icy blue opals of his eyes catching the room's pale light. "So it did happen." I gently jigged the baby as if he was alive. "What's your plan?"

"Now we'll see if you pass the test," he said, walking away.

He left me with the baby. I shivered with my back to the open freezer. When I sensed he wasn't returning, I placed the baby inside and closed the lid. I sat on the freezer with my back against the wall. It was the first time in so long that I heard nothing at all. The silence was soon interrupted by the burst of burning gas from the metal spool, an enormous Bunsen burner of sorts, with a flow of green flames, the layers of it saturating towards pure white. In the center, I saw the faint, ghostly impression of Bobby's grinning mouth. I walked to the flame and he leapt on top of it, letting it burn through his belly, fractals of emerald cinders curling above.

"Get out of there!" I said.

His grin never faded, and as the flames continued to burn, I saw that they spared him from combustion. Leaning out flat on the spool, his fingertips reached for me. The flame's dry, aggressive heat danced on the flesh until our hands, still cold, were entwined. He got on his knees so the flames rose up around his whole body.

"What is this?" I asked.

"Ingredient One for our séance," he said.

"Séance? What for?"

"We're gonna call Kev."

"And the other ingredients?"

"Just one more: a witch's first-born."

"Wow. Are you sure you want me here?"

His lips twitched through a range of excited smiles. "I want you as close as I can get you."

My skin itched with discomfort, but I trusted that I wouldn't burn. I pounced on top of him and the flames reached around our stomachs. It hurt, like holding a match beneath your palm, but no more than that. It served only to excite us. The pain clouded the sensation of his hands creeping up beneath my t-shirt and pushing it off. I did the same with his, and somehow, aside from all else, I could feel the warmth of our skin together, like the heat was not a single gradient but my body was a tongue tasting its many flavours. The touch of our skin was so sweet. I had the first two buttons of his jeans' fly undone when I heard the voices, saw their torchlight waving across the ceiling.

"Up here's where I did my best work," a voice said. "Hey! What are you guys doing up here?" It was Hugo! "Mum," he said, "we should probably…"

"Boys!"

We rolled off the spool and ducked behind it. Bobby extinguished the flames. I felt around the bare concrete for my t-shirt. It had soaked in something, so I left it.

"What are you doing here?" Mum said, gathering up the folds of her draping shawl.

"I think it's pretty clear," Hugo said, laughing.

"I don't mean that," she said. "It's not safe here."

"Why are you here?" I said.

"Your brother wanted to show me his latest pieces," she said. "He's not doing this where he's not wanted. This building's abandoned, and it really does look brighter. He's a great artist."

"Another time, I guess," Hugo said.

"Sure," Mum said. "You kids must be freezing."

Bobby and I sat in the back seat of Mum's car, on either side of Hugo, who lent me his jacket and Bobby his cardigan.

"Cheers," Bobby said as we arrived at his house and he hopped out.

Hugo got into the front seat and Mum continued to drive us home.

"You guys are like brothers," she said.

"*Like* brothers?" Hugo said. "We are. Right?"

"Not you two." She caught my eye in the rear-view mirror. "You and Bobby."

The next night, just as I began drifting off, I heard a crunch outside and looked to see Mum's car mangled in the driveway.

"No!" Mum was soon in the hall, yelling. "This is too much. You don't pay rent, you've crashed my car, you're on drugs again."

"Stop acting like a dick," Hugo said.

"I never would've spoken to my mother like that! I'm not letting you back in this house. You've blown it, son. Now fuck off."

The arguments seeped through the walls while I lay in my bed, pillows wrapped around my head. Some part of me refused to switch off, and I couldn't help but tune into what was going on down below.

I wanted to sleep so badly. The whimpering came through the stained windowpane. Hugo scraped his nails across the washboard formation of glass grapes: scratch, scratch. I could see him in my mind with those big druggy bug eyes like a little lost child, so I went to him.

"Sam," he said. His face looked bruised through the coloured glass.

"Hey, Hugo." I turned the doorknob and he fell on top of me, his ruddy cheeks cold against mine. With a baby's primal confusion, he cried, wailing for someone to find him, diagnose his woes and quell them. "You're okay," I said, stroking his hair.

"Sam!" Mum said, coming back from the living room. "We're not letting him back in."

"Do you want him to go the way of Kev?" I said. "You know what's going to happen if he leaves tonight."

"Maeve's boy?" Mum said. "What happened to him?"

"You didn't know?"

"Time to go, Hugo."

I held a hand out. "There was a time when you were happy he was alive. The terror of thinking he'd be born dead. Years of hearing that croup cough. How else do you expect him to act? Look at him." I rolled him off me, towards the radiator, along which he slinked like a human draught excluder. "He's that same baby. And if you let him leave, he won't be able to fend for himself. What he did to your car... we're lucky he came back alive tonight. You really wanna risk sending him back out again?"

"I don't care," she said, "and I would've thought with how he's persecuted you, you'd support me."

I stood up and shut the front door. "I thought I'd want this too. But you changed my mind."

"I did?"

"I wanna show you something."

Mum climbed up the ladder first and I followed. There was Bobby again, fully clothed this time, standing between three orbs, which formed an equilateral triangle of light around the room's metal spool. I walked up and kissed him on the cheek.

"Is she coming?" I said.

"She should be here by now," he said.

"What's going on, boys?" Maeve said. "Why did you want me to...?" Her head appeared in the floor's square hole.

"Bobby and I have something we want to show you both," I said.

Maeve paced up beside Mum and they stood watching us with concern.

"Go stand over there with your mum, Sam," he said. He knelt down before the furnace and brought his palms together in front of his head, closing his eyes as the hands came down to split the image of his face in two. There was an audible rush of gas, which brought the flames into being.

Placing his hands on the furnace's rim, he began to hum one note after another in a pattern. The pentatonic scale, maybe, or a repeated devil's interval. A full circle of green flames grew and curled towards themselves in a loose spiral like the petals of a gentle peony. He hummed harder, his brow sweaty, and the flame petals shivered, vibrating with such intensity that they blended as they grew.

"Get back!"

A tower of green shot to the ceiling and spread out in fronds, into a tree of light.

"What's happening?" I asked, but din of the burning furnace drowned my words. We fell back and away from the heat, shutting our eyes tightly. When the light dimmed, I opened my eyes and saw two holograms in the flames. One was Kevin. The other I didn't know.

"Adam," Mum said. "That's him, right? Adam, is that you?"

"Hi," Adam said.

"Bobby, this isn't funny!" Maeve said. "What is this?"

"It's me, Mum," Kev said.

"You sound like... I've missed you so much, Kev. Why did you have to do it?"

"What did he do?" Mum said, "Did he...? Oh, Maeve." They hugged, sobbed.

Mum tried to mop up her tears with her soaking sleeves. "Adam, why did you do it?"

"You want the pupil answer?" he said, and he laughed.

"Give them some time," Bobby said softly, taking my hand and guiding us to the freezer, where we sat with our knees to our chests, watching our mothers through the pale green flames.

"I'm so glad this worked out," I said.

He kissed the back of my hand. 'me too."

"I'm never leaving you, you know."

"I know."

While reading the last lines of his diary, Sam called Maeve on his mobile. When she picked up, he'd become feverishly unintelligible.

"Sam, tell me what's going on," she said. Ingrained reflexes brought back her mother's calming tone effortlessly.

"The flames," he said, "the green flames!"

"I remember," she said and added, awakened, "Oh God! How did we ever forget?"

Sam shook his head, body slumping over itself. "He made us," he said. "I can't figure out why. But tonight, from each death, a new clue. It wants us to go there."

"You're not making any sense. When I saw you earlier, I was worried. You don't look good, Sam. You live in that flat by yourself with too much time to think. It's not healthy."

She heard only static-flecked whimpering.

"It's late, Sam. Go to bed. I'm free tomorrow. We'll meet in the café again and talk, okay? This is like that call from Kev! Is that what you're going to let this be like? Listen to me, Sam. God knows I've lost a lot of people. And so have you. We'll be okay. Go to sleep, Sam. Meet me in the morning! Sam!"

The phone line went dead.

"Christ!"

A tunnel of wind blew through the building, which had cleared out the squatters from a decade ago. More walls had crumbled, and those that remained held Hugo and Bobby's names only in the palimpsest of their spray's bumps beneath the white paint that had erased all their colors and images. The freezer was still there. It had been turned on its side and laid open, corroding. The furnace had also survived years of ravaging weather, and before it knelt Sam, in joggers and a hoody.

"You shouldn't have come back here," she said.

"Do you remember the tune he sang?" He hummed. "I was never much of a singer." He turned and lunged at her, grabbing her roughly by the shoulders, his expression one of pouting rage. "He was your son! Whatever gift he had, you must have given it to him. You taught him the melody, right? Sing it for me!"

"Why do you think we forgot?" she said, on the border of composure. "Bobby made a mistake. He was never supposed to show us what he did. He must have been using his power all those years to block it from our memories. I never should've given you his diary."

"He's dead! Why should he decide what we get to see?" he said, turning away from her and kneeling by the furnace again. "Don't you want to see him?"

"I wish he was still alive," she said. "That's not the same. You said it yourself on the phone. Tonight, you went on a journey of death. Where do you expect it to lead?"

He shimmied around the furnace, the wind numbing him from feeling the keen pressure in his knees—skin against the bone and concrete, the metal stealing the warmth from his fingers. "What does it need?" he said.

"What *you* need is to go home!" she said. "If you ever cared about anyone in my family, or your own, you'll take them with you as best you can and go on and live a good life. You were never supposed to see them again."

"Why not?" Gritting his teeth hard, he couldn't stop the pain purging from his mouth in a bitter roar.

"I don't know, Sam," she said, walking towards him and placing a hand on his shoulder. He looked to see many rings on all her fingers shining softly and leaned his head against her arm. "You've lost so much. I know it hurts. I know." She stood by him and stroked his shoulder while he recovered, paying no mind to the oddly sexual *hmm* sounds he began to make, considering them a by-product of grief's primality. The humming got louder and formed a tune from some bygone memory.

Maeve retracted her hand from him. He was burning, his skin glowing green. He slumped over the furnace, arms in a loose circle around its rim, humming still, until a match head-sized flame bloomed from its center. As he hummed louder, the flame expanded. It was hollow, its glowing shell masking the portal forming inside it. He bashed his fists on the furnace's rim and the flame opened up like a Venus flytrap in reverse. Flakes of old ashes rose lazily from the portal, filling the air with the pungent smell of a dying fire.

Maeve edged up against the wall, peering into the portal and seeing a world of dust, a maze of bodies running like cattle through its grey, charcoal plane of thunderous footsteps and aching moans.

The unveiled doorway grew with Sam's invitation to rip out a rift. His eyes closed and he dipped into a frozen, automatic state as the portal ate the floor beneath him, swallowing him up.

Dear Hugo,

I just got back from Sam's funeral. I guess you didn't manage to make it. Well, we've both been to enough of these and I want to be honest about it for once. Do you feel the same way about them as I do? That no matter what people say—even if, miraculously, what they say has nothing to do with making someone else's death all about themselves—it just seems to make things worse? Yet, the worst they could say is nothing?

Anyway, I just wanted to thank you for being honest last time we met. I really was about to call Martha that summer. I thought she and I were in tune, that we'd carry on our summer tradition of meeting for lovely dinners in that big back garden of your family home. I knew she was ill of course, because she stopped coming to school. But I didn't know it was terminal. I'm sorry you had to lie for her, to tell me she was okay. I still don't totally understand it.

The night Sam went missing, I went back to his flat to work out what had gotten him so fired up. I traced his reading material back from his own diary to yours to Bobby's, which I'd given him that afternoon. The only conclusion I can make—and I hope you don't think I'm crazy for saying so—is that some force was seducing him, and wanted to claim him. We took part for sure, but please don't think you did anything wrong. This was something far more compelling than either of us had a chance of fighting against.

It reminded me of something. I know you remember there was a kid called Adam in your mum's class who committed suicide. It threw her into the worst depression I'd ever seen. I urged her to get professional help, but after a single appointment with a psychiatrist, she came to me, rambling on about the uselessness of therapy, how she was so much smarter than the woman she'd met with, who'd deigned to ask Martha what she was like when she was

Adam's age. That question was the very reason she refused to return.

Martha saw herself in Adam. Her further years on the planet allowed her to feel the weight of everything he'd extinguished with his death. She thought of her wonderful life, her kids, and was met with the horror that none of it might have happened if she hadn't had the strength to survive her teenage years. None of you would have existed, provided her with so many happy memories, or gone on to start families of your own.

Hugo, I don't know why we have to keep going, and I don't yet know how we will. But we can't give in.

Maeve

HARDENED HEARTS

PORCELAIN SKIN

LAURA BLACKWELL

Ruth was weeding the vegetable garden when her grandnephew's ridiculous tiny car crunched the driveway gravel. She stood and stretched her back, wondering whether he would commend her work ethic or instead lecture her about overdoing it.

Instead, Michael held a wooden box out to her. "I met an old family friend the other day," he said, beaming.

Ruth stared at the unfamiliar thing. It was bigger than a recipe box, smaller than a shoe box, and made of heavily polished rosewood. "All right," she said cautiously.

Michael's smile slipped. "It's from Helen's son. He wants you to have it. You remember Helen, right?"

"Helen was my best friend," snapped Ruth. "She died in 1982. It's been thirteen years, but I haven't forgotten her." Never forgot the gentle smile, the scent of her lily-of-the-valley soap.

"He said this was on her dresser as long as he could remember," Michael explained, looking disappointed. "He thought maybe you gave it to her, because you two used to go to the ballet together in Atlanta."

Michael opened the box lid, and a porcelain dancer sprang into view, slowly rotating to a tinkling tune.

Ruth shook her head. Not even the tune was familiar. "If it was Helen's, I'd be honored to have it. I'll write him a thank-you note later today."

Ruth and Michael had lunch at the one restaurant that changed the oil for the fried okra often enough. Afterward, he checked the noisy pipe in the bathroom, but didn't find a leak to repair. By midafternoon, the stunted rear of his toy-like car was turned to her house, and the gravel crunched for what was likely to be the last time until the electric-meter reader came. The closest neighbor was a quarter of a mile away.

When she went to bed that night, Ruth wound the music box and set it on her bedside table. She watched the pretty ballerina spin slowly. The minor-key tune wasn't from a ballet; it sounded more like a lullaby. The pink satin lining told her nothing, nor did the ballerina's pose (arms in sixth position, feet *en pointe* in first), nor did the oval mirror that doubled its movement. Ruth examined the serene porcelain face, with its softly blushing cheeks, its pink smile, its direct gaze. People used to say Helen had porcelain skin—and to be sure, it wasn't freckled and sun-roughened like Ruth's—but the ballerina was a different thing altogether. It was new to her, nothing to remind her of her friend, but Ruth felt a surge of warmth toward it anyway.

Ruth's blankets fell away, and she couldn't find them in the stuffy dark. She strained to hear the tune of the music box, but it was lost in a sea of delicate, glassy sounds. Instead of touching her well-worn cotton sheets, her feet brushed across velvet. She sat up and focused on the thread of the plaintive tune she'd heard before falling asleep. Surely she was asleep.

The melody had words, words sung in the clear, quiet voice of a woman who expects only one person to hear her.

Come to me
Through the trees
Bearing gemstone fruit

Jewels bright
Velvet night
I will sing the truth of you

Ruth lurched to a stand and looked around, assessing the tall shapes looming out of the darkness. As her eyes adjusted, she recognized them as trees. As color and detail returned, she saw that the trees' bark was black velvet, and that their branches dripped with amulets of protection: a blue glass pendant with a brown eye in its center, a carved maybe-Chinese woman with one hand raised, a gold medal cast with the image of a saint whose name she'd forgotten. A perimeter to protect against intruders, perhaps.

The trees let Ruth pass among them, past their velvet trunks and under their satin leaves. No animals moved in the forest and the only sound was the chiming of ornaments swaying sedately together in the breezeless night. The amulets gave way to other jewels: carnelian persimmons, peaches carved from pale jade, clusters of amethyst grapes. She plucked a grape and tasted it, or tried to; it was cool and crisp in her mouth, but dissolved without sweetness.

At the center of a clearing ringed with these trees of jewel-fruits, the ballerina from the box, now the size of a living woman, rotated slowly on a pedestal. Ruth had to lift her chin to see the ballerina's entire face and saw that it was the same, gentle despite the lofty height. Her face filled Ruth with both peace and longing. Then fear gripped Ruth as she realized that the ballerina was slowing down.

Ruth hurried around the base of the pedestal, looking for what had to be there... yes, there it was, the key that would wind the ballerina again. She cranked it with both hands, listening to hear the now-wordless tune return to its proper pace.

"I hope you're all right," Ruth said aloud. She should have felt foolish, talking to a porcelain statue whose face showed no response, but she didn't. She wished she could climb up on to the pedestal and wrap an arm around the ballerina's waist, dance a few steps of a *pas des deux* with her. But there was no way to be sure that any sound she heard was an answer, so Ruth kept the question inside, instead observing, "I think you're the queen of this place." With that, Ruth went to explore the rest of the queen's domain.

The forest petered out at the edge of a sea. As she approached it, Ruth saw that the waves were ripples of blue satin, the whitecaps glittering diamond rings. So many tokens of love and devotion, all tumbling together and indistinct, each little more than a drop in an ocean. Helen had accepted a diamond ring from a man, and it took Ruth months to understand why the sparkle on Helen's hand and the sparkle in her eye made her heart plummet.

The wordless tune drew Ruth back to the forest clearing, and she sat watching the ballerina's carefully turned feet, her expressive hands, her elegant chin. Every angle presented a new view of wonderment and beauty, like a waterfall full of rainbows.

Although the air remained close and still, the sky shifted gradually, its deep blue velvet changing to satin, its diamond stars transmuting into sundogs. It started in a direction that might have been east, the sun brilliant and blinding and strangely oval. The mirror inside the music box. Ruth stole one last glance over her shoulder at the ballerina queen, then walked through the forest to the bright shape. She awoke under her own faded quilt in her own queen-size bed, which felt slightly too large, although she had never shared it with anyone.

Ruth harvested a few cherry tomatoes before the day's heat grew overwhelming, then sat on her porch nursing a cup of tea. On a typical July day, she enjoyed this view: the drooping white blossoms of the sourwood tree a graceful touch against the pines and hickories of the woods and the Blue Ridge Mountains rising proud beyond. That day, though, the ballerina's serene smile and gracefully turned hands floated into her mind's eye. The ballerina's slender fingers were fused together. They would never accept a diamond ring.

Ruth went about her chores by rote, and ate out of habit rather than hunger. Instead of reading or watching TV, Ruth dealt a hand of solitaire and reshuffled methodically, unable to concentrate. There was no one to visit or call on the phone. She had never expected to live alone this long.

It was a relief to slip away into the bejeweled world again that night, and she made her way quickly to the ballerina queen's clearing. After making sure the music-box mechanism was wound tight, Ruth sat down. Hands absently stroking the velvet of the forest floor, she watched the soft light gleam off the ballerina's slender arms and muscled shoulders.

Once, Ruth asked, "What is your name?" but heard no answer in the tinkling music. Ruth would not presume to name the queen. Nor did she presume to touch her, either in the velvet world or in her own.

Ruth awoke refreshed and clean, her hair unmussed.

Ruth returned the next night and the night after that. The ballerina was always the same, constant as the diamond stars. Though Ruth was never hungry in the music-box world, she sampled a golden-scaled fish, raw like the ceviche she wouldn't try even when Michael made it. It tasted of nothing, just as the coral roses smelled of nothing.

She could never feel bored looking on the graceful queen of the realm, but Ruth wanted something more. One night, she tucked a miniature volume of May Sarton's poetry into the music box, and was delighted to find it waiting for her by the ballerina's pedestal. Ruth read a few of her favorites aloud to the ballerina. They sometimes fell into the rhythm of the lullaby and sometimes contrasted with it, but Ruth thought that all in all, the words and the sounds added something to the place. She hoped that the ballerina was pleased.

When the light from the oval brightened that morning, Ruth set the book next to the faint depression her body was beginning to leave in the velvet. The book's worn cover and yellowed pages looked shabby and out of place there; all the magic was in the words, and that magic was strongest when spoken.

When she returned that evening, the book was still there, solid and silent. Ruth knew she was welcome.

"Is there anything I can do to help you?" Ruth asked the ballerina queen. She listened for a voice on the bell-like notes of music box.

If you keep
The key to me
I will dance eternally

Ruth tugged at the music-box key and learned that it was not detachable. To remove it would be to destroy the mechanism. "Then I'm like a lighthouse-keeper," she said aloud. "That's more than a full-time job."

As the ballerina turned, her immobile face showed Ruth sympathy, then hope, then anticipation. She would make no demands of Ruth, just as Ruth made none of her.

"I'm not sure I like your world," Ruth admitted, "but I'm not sure I care for mine anymore, either. And I do know I could stare into your face forever."

Then please do

And I'll sing the truth of you

Ruth did not wait for another evening. Fully awake, fully conscious, she filled the music box with the things she might miss: a deck of cards, a rolled-up pair of slippers, a tomato plant carefully dug up from the garden. She picked up a playbill from a ballet she'd seen with Helen, a superb *Giselle*, but set it aside. That time in her life was over.

The music box wasn't full, but Ruth had all she wanted. She lay down on top of the bedspread, the box on her chest. She couldn't bring herself to touch the ballerina. Whether the porcelain was solid or hollow, warm or cold, was not for Ruth to learn without asking—and Ruth had always been shy to ask about matters of the body and the heart.

Ruth touched the mirror with both hands and found herself kneeling at the feet of the ballerina's pedestal. A light breeze accompanied her, making the jewel-fruits clack and chime.

The ballerina continued her stately, frozen dance. Ruth wound the key and stood back, admiring the sheen of the ballerina's glazed skin under the mirror's bright sunlight.

"We both know the truth of me," Ruth told the ballerina, her queen. "You don't need to sing it now. It may take me a while, but please let me say it first."

Ruth didn't count the days and nights between her arrival and the moment Michael's worried face appeared in the mirror. His hands sifted the treasures she'd left in the box and his face crumpled. He had no way of knowing where she was, that she was safe and content.

When Michael closed the box, the deck of cards plummeted to the velvet ground beside her. The slippers bounced when they landed, and the tomato plant, now withered, fell in a shower of dry dirt. Ruth would have liked to taste tomatoes again, but she had all the nourishment necessary, and she was glad to have something more of home. Her cards, her slippers, and her book of poems were all she needed to feel that she had moved in, that she belonged.

Ruth stretched out on the black velvet, staring up at the ballerina. Her porcelain queen's gentle face and graceful limbs were beautiful beyond compare. She would never age, never change, never give herself to another.

It would never be too late for Ruth to tell the music-box ballerina what was in her all-too-human heart.

HARDENED HEARTS

THE HEART OF THE ORCHARD
ERIN SWEET AL-MEHAIRI

Melissa looked outside the small, shuttered window, feeling the warm breeze on her face, breathing in the scent of the outdoors. Winding a strand of her shiny, black hair around her finger till it spiraled like a snake, she stared at the row of fruit trees, lost deep in thought.

She lived in a cozy cottage, once a guesthouse, on the big estate of the McPhersons. The entire property had been in Melissa's family for generations until her dad, Tom, had died in a freak accident and her mother alone couldn't support the ancestral wine and fruit farm business of her dad's family. When her mother, Mary Jane, sold the land to the McPhersons, both of them had been in tears. Melissa felt, as they all did, that once your roots are planted on a land for so long, it claims you for its own.

Luckily, the McPhersons were old family friends who owned an adjacent farm. Her mother moved in with her aging grandmother an hour south, where she was originally from before she had met Melissa's father one summer at a regional farmer's market. In their kindness, the McPhersons had invited Melissa to stay and turn the guesthouse, with its petite orchard plot, into a cottage all her own. The larger house they would will to their own daughter Eve later in life, if she wanted it, and would continue to live on their own farm. They undertook the larger wine and fruit business of Melissa's family and she would help them seasonally, especially at the beginning, since she knew the land well. The small orchard would be enough for her to produce fruit to take to the local farm markets to keep herself afloat. She was like a daughter to them; she had spent many days of her childhood hanging out with Mr. and Mrs. McPherson, Eve, and her brother, Nic. Ever since she was a little girl, her family had kept the McPhersons stocked with pickings of fruit for Margorie McPherson's famous pies.

Of course, there was a shameful, unspoken reason that they had thrown her this bone—not everything can be perfect in life, can it? Melissa tried not to dwell on the reason for their kindness in gifting her the quaint, stone cottage, with its red front door, bronzed gnome-faced door knocker, and yellow flowers that peeked their heads out of sky blue, wooden-slatted window boxes. She just tried to move on as best she could, seeking solace in nature and her plot of land.

Nic had been her first true love since she was fourteen. By the time they were both sixteen, he had wanted to move quicker than she did. She grew up with her parents instilling in her the importance of saving herself for marriage, and though she hoped Nic was the one, she wasn't at all ready for either of those things. But just kissing wasn't enough for him.

One night, after a movie with Nic and his family, she had been walking back home on a well-worn path that cut through the forest that connected both farms and families. Nic appeared suddenly from behind a tree and attacked her, violently hitting her head against a tree, throwing her down forcefully, and raping her as she cried "no" alone into the night, eventually succumbing to her own whimpering and the shame. Afterwards, suddenly alarmed his own ferociousness, he looked at her in horror and ran back into the trees.

She limped home, her white blouse torn, khaki shorts ripped at the seam, blood seeping from the wound on her head, and with scratches on her knees. There was no way to hide this horrible incident from her mother, who always waited up for her at the kitchen table with a glass of Ovaltine and a goodnight hug. That night, her mother embraced her in an even tighter hug, and after she had wiped her tears away, bandaged Melissa's head and knees as best she could (Melissa pleaded frantically for her mother to not call the ambulance and local sheriff), she grabbed the lantern and set off to the McPhersons, outraged. Meanwhile, Melissa sank down onto the couch, her legs pulled up underneath her, and rocked herself to sleep, feeling a pain far beyond the physical.

Nic had been sent away to an uncle's house in the city, with regrets to Melissa and her mother. The McPhersons wanted to keep it quiet, of course, and Melissa didn't want to press charges even though her mother, and a lawyer that her mother consulted against her wishes, were pressuring her for justice. Since her mother was in financial trouble already, a deal was made instead. It didn't matter to Melissa, as her heart was forever broken beyond repair. No court judgment would change that, just as they could never exact enough revenge on Nic. She'd rather her family be helped through her pain Her Dad had already been gone for a few years, so with the amount of money the McPhersons agreed to pay for their farm (an amount padded over its market value), the transfer was made.

Now, as she stared out her window, the morning sun shone on her face and glinted off the leaves on the row of peach trees in front of her. Light could play tricks, so she had to take a double look—but yes, she saw something moving between the trees. Not something, but someone. A short, stout man, his head just gracing the bottom layer of the leaves under a peach tree, laid back against the trunk with his arms crossed and his legs the same, one foot over the other. His boots were large for his stature, his white beard a little unkempt, and his dark eyes piercing and barely visible under the rim of an oversized gray hat.

"Hey, what are you doing on my property?" she yelled out to the man, once startled awake from her daydreaming enough to speak. With the looks of the fellow, she wondered if she was still dreaming.

"Your trees need fertilized," he said, very matter-of-factly. Snapping his fingers, he waved over the trees. "If you want a better, bigger fruit, you'll need to remedy this for harvest next year."

"Who are you and why do you care?" Melissa asked, dumbfounded that this man would dare to tell her how to grow peaches, even if over the years they had been decreasing in size. Nervousness crept into her voice and she asked, "Do you work for the McPhersons?"

"Oh, no," he said, more gently. "I don't work for anyone. But I did hear at the farmer's market that the McPhersons pick fruit from a secret orchard. Mrs. McPherson promises better pies, the best in the state, putting them on the map as a travel destination."

"It's my family's legacy to grow the best pie peaches for miles around," she offered, putting her hands on her hips and biting her lower lip. "They wouldn't have planted another orchard so close without me knowing. She gets all hers from me."

"Oh, but they did, my dear," he reiterated. "I've seen them, tasted a peach or two, up on the hill on the far side after dark, no one the wiser."

"That can't be..." she started.

"Oh, yes it can. Almost as juicy and deliciously sweet as yours, perhaps a might tastier," he said with a saccharine smile.

She ran her hand through her straight hair, which she wore down with no frills or fuss. She didn't even know this strange man and here she was caught up in his words. But her peaches... she had to do all she could to preserve their superior quality and far-reaching renown. It's all she had. Now that she thought about it, Mrs. McPherson hadn't been over as often to get fruit this season. Could they be harvesting their own fruit? She thought for a few minutes on the possibility, but the man cut into her focus.

"Let me assist you, Melissa," he said, his soft eyes bearing something intangible and preternatural. "I've stayed hidden for hundreds of years. I am an orchard man, created centuries ago by the fruit trees, and when a need is recognized, I listen. I am a part of the trees and this land as much as you are. I know about the terrible night in the forest. I heard the abominable act, and your stilted screams of shock, from high up in a branch, but there was nothing I could do. I wasn't in human form at the time."

"W-what?" she stammered at him, not comprehending what he was saying. "That is a tall tale if I ever heard one. I wouldn't believe you at all if it weren't for the fact you know about what happened to me. From whom, I don't know, but you must have heard about it at the market. Someone is spreading rumors."

"Believe me or not, it's true," he said, and took two small steps toward her. "But what have you got to lose by listening to me? You don't want them to compete with your small peach orchard, do you? Will you let them win? I can see you need some support and I truly want to help you."

She fluttered her eyelashes, not moving an inch otherwise, not saying a word. She was almost frozen in fear.

"Look. I have a secret herb," he confessed, pulling two pouches from his moss green, over-sized coat pocket. "If you drink it each time right before you go to bed, you will feel replenished in the morning. I can tell you haven't been sleeping well. Tossing and turning, sometimes waking up panicked or alarmed, right? It's natural when you've suffered trauma, but this will calm you. Also," he held out the second pouch, "here is a special mixture to fertilize the trees in the morning. This fertilizer will create peaches unlike any you've seen. There is no way a rival could compare. Consider it a boost to your already wonderful fruit."

She considered what he was saying, and though he was a little odd, she found his energy nearing undeniable, maybe uncanny, with a meandering gypsy sort of quality. He was right too. She was very tired most days, waking up often from night sweats, nightmares, and a battle with insomnia. Adding the news that the McPhersons were secretly trying to compete with her peaches, after everything else she had went through due to their son, was almost too much for her to handle. This little traveler and his concoctions were worth a try. After all, what more did she have to lose?

Melissa took the golden pouch he extended to her with the herb concoction to help her sleep, and then the black one, which held small granules for fertilizing the trees. Turning to go into the house, she told him thank you, offering a weary smile. He grinned at her, and said, "It's my pleasure, my dear. Now I'm off, to sell seeds and plants, and advice, since I have a... let's say... background... in alchemy, but I am happy to provide my tested remedies to lovely ladies in need for free."

"Where do you stay, as a… a traveling salesman?" she asked him, curious as she knew no motels or hotels in any sort of likely radius.

"I don't need much to sleep. I am a wanderer, one with the forests and orchards, and I sleep wherever I can. I pick a tree and plop under it," he said with a wink. Now you know of my existence, it's only right I ask if you would mind if I slept near your orchard? There is a fine spot toward the backside."

"Sleep in the orchard? Outside…? I…" she trailed off with a nod of her head indicating yes to him. Then, she went inside as the sun was glowing a vibrant orange, the sky around it tinged with pink and purple cotton candy swirls, the orb dropping slowly down under the horizon. She checked the deadbolt, twice, just in case.

Melissa steeped the herbs in hot water and drank a good portion of it, grabbed her book of fairy tales (wondering for a second if she had been reading too many of these for her own good), and went to the couch. She was fast asleep before she had turned three pages. The book fell out of her hand, onto the floor with a thud, but she didn't hear it.

As the sun's rays shone blindingly through the living room curtains, causing dust motes to explode awake, Melissa rubbed her eyes, realized she was lying curled up in a ball on the couch. She had fallen asleep in her cotton, flowery print dress from the night before. She looked down at her feet as she was about to rise. Her bare feet were a little more dirty than usual. She wondered if when she ran outside yesterday to talk to the man in the orchard she had forgotten to slip on her shoes? That must be it, but she couldn't fully remember. She took a quick shower, and by the time she had dressed in her jean shorts and aqua tank top, she pined for a hot cup of caffeine. She was thankful her cottage was made of stone as it always stayed cool in the mornings on warm days.

As she cupped her mug, cream-colored with I am WOMAN Hear Me Roar written in red script on the outside, she mused about how much those herbs in her tea last night quelled her nerves, because she remembered nothing at all, not even her dreams, if she'd had any. And she felt more awake than she had in a long time. She ran her hand through her damp hair, and sighed. I better put this new energy to work today, she thought.

She set her mug in the sink and noticed one of her large, serrated knives in the dish drainer. Did I cut zucchini last night for dinner? she mumbled to herself. She enjoyed frying it up fresh from her garden plot, with onions, garlic, and butter, and it was a fair assumption she had eaten it. The act of chopping vegetables for dinner was great stress relief.

She looked into the refrigerator, but there were no leftovers in a plastic container as usual to prompt her memory. Those herbs certainly had given her a fresh start this morning, she thought, just like the man in the orchard had said.

Melissa's long, lean fingers opened the shutters above the kitchen sink; she closed her eyes and her dainty nose breathed in the orchard air. Always a hint of sweetness to the breeze that she loved, this had become a regular morning ritual. She opened her round eyes to a start. The Orchard Man was under a tree close to the window, reading a book.

"Morning, young lass, did you sleep well?" he said with a glimmer in his eye.

"I haven't slept that well in many years," she said. "Thank you so much for the herbs."

"My pleasure," he said. "I'll be off now to sell my seeds. Don't forget to sprinkle those vitamins I gave you near the root of your trees!"

Melissa walked row by row with the pouch, scattering the mixture near the bottom of each tree trunk. As she came to the tenth row, she noticed the last tree trunk had newly dug dirt nearby. What rodent was digging near her trees now? Two years ago, groundhogs had been trying to dig homes through the orchard. She had to keep an eye out again.

The rest of her day was spent around the farm until late afternoon when she drove her yellow Volkswagen Beetle into the Sunday Farmer's Market. On Sundays they had their after mart, where vegetables and fruit, not sold on Saturday morning, were available at a lower cost for the late afternoon crowd. Many vendors brought fresh items though as well, knowing that sometimes people couldn't make it to shop on Saturday mornings. One of those vendors was Mrs. Olivia Burk, who always brought Melissa a dozen eggs to last her the week. In the mornings, Melissa made herself omelets, just like her Daddy used to make, with sautéed fresh mushrooms, chives, and the ripest tomatoes on top. She missed her dad more than ever and omelets were a simple way for her stay close to him.

Melissa smiled at Mrs. Burk, a plump fifty-year-old woman with narrow, blue eyes and a jovial nature. She was always in an apron and a flowing skirt, with her hair in a bun on the top of her head. "Did you hear, Melissa?" Mrs. Burk crowed, as she released her from a tight hug. She continued in a hushed tone, "A young boy was found murdered last night out on Old Post Road. Only sixteen and... and... worst of all... someone c-cut his heart from his chest!"

"W-What?" Melissa was shocked at such an especially heinous thing happening in their little county. She waited for her heart to skip a beat, speeding up with fear, but it didn't. "How sad for his family," she said finally, biting at her nails. Mrs. Burk lowered her head and nodded in agreement. They paused in silence for a moment. "That's a horrendous way to die," Melissa said, finally. "Was it an animal?" she questioned. They had so much forestland surrounding them with multiple accounts of bear, coyote, and cougars.

"They aren't sure yet," Mrs. Burk said, then stroked Melissa's arm like a mother. "But yes, either way, it's a sad day. You be careful when you're out walking sweetie, especially at night."

Melissa spent the next week feeling much better overall from the herbs and the increased sleep. She continued to sprinkle the fertilizer under the trees every morning and the Orchard Man greeted her warmly each day before going his own way.

The trees were bearing not only more fruit, but the peaches themselves had doubled in diameter. Even though she was feeling more normal, and was ecstatic about the fruit, she still worried about her memory loss. Her clothes from the day before were sometimes on the line outside hanging with clothespins as if they had been hand-washed and left to dry in the wind, while the rest of the laundry remained in the bin awaiting weekly washings at the laundromat, and a few times, the ax from the red shed out back had been propped up by the back door. She found that odd, as she always returned it to the barn after cutting wood and that was only in the winter.

The next Sunday was a bright, clear day and she decided to walk to the Farmer's After Mart instead of driving. It was no problem for her to walk the distance, about a mile or two, and the temperature was perfect. It would give her a chance to clear her head, at least it usually did. Feeling the sun on her face, watching the fields and trees change colors with the seasons, she loved the serenity of wide, open spaces. Long walks and jogging helped her cope with the stress after the attack. However, this time before she even made it halfway there, she clutched at the pain in her chest. There was pressure on her heart and she became short of breath, breaking out in a sweat. Once she made it to the market, she sat on a bench right outside the tented vendor area.

"Melissa, are you okay?" Mrs. Burk's voice called out to her from inside the tent. "You look pale." The aging lady came out to see her with a harried look on her face.

"For some odd reason, I was having chest pains as I walked here," she recounted.

After sitting and talking for a few minutes about the symptoms, Mrs. Burk fetched Melissa a water bottle from another vendor, and then set back down by her. "Maybe you are just a little dehydrated today. Drink some water and rest a bit. I can drive you home," Mrs. Burk offered.

"You're probably right," she said, after taking a big swig of the water. "I have been feeling so much better otherwise, sleeping better and all, so hopefully this is a one-time occurrence."

"I'm glad, after what you've been through. I can barely sleep myself with this murderer lurking about," Mrs. Burk exclaimed as she ran her fingers across her throat gently. "The number of murdered boys is up to seven and I am scared for my own son, Joshua." She began to tear up. "I don't know what I'd do if I lost him, he's only nineteen and my youngest. And I can't even begin to fathom if it happened as brutally as the other boys. In some cases, I've heard, they were attacked with an ax to the chest cavity. What reason would someone have to be savagely ripping these boys to pieces and stealing their hearts? Cut them right out of their chests? Oh, I can't even think about it a moment longer."

Melissa shook her head from side to side. She wished she had a Kleenex to offer Mrs. Burk, but the lady just pulled her apron up and blew her nose loudly on a patch above the hem. Melissa didn't want to think about the murders any longer either so she stayed quiet. She continued to bite the skin around her nails, even though she had already taken the nails down to nubs. She took a drink of her water and patted Mrs. Burk on the arm. This time it was her turn to console the woman, though she was hardly in a position to do so.

"Let me get your eggs and drive you home then," Mrs. Burk said, sniffling. "I think you need to lie down. I can see it in your face."

"I think you're right, but I think you might need to take a break yourself, Mrs. Burk. I know you're worried, but I'm sure Joshua will be fine," she said.

After she got home, she waved to the Orchard Man. He roamed amidst the peach trees, examining the leaves and the fruit. She walked over to him and asked if the chest pains she was experiencing could be a side effect of the herbs he had given her for restful sleep.

"Usually, no," he said, slowly and methodically. "But perhaps, though you're sleeping, your heartache lingers, you know, underneath it all. The herbs don't heal all that anger and hurt. They help you sleep better. Are you sure it's physical pain, or does it just feel that way?" He glanced at her and his pupils dilated, but she looked off toward the horizon in thought.

She didn't speak further, so he quickly said, "But your peaches are growing lovely, my dear. Large, juicy, colorful, and very sweet. Those pies I smell you baking must taste delicious." He rubbed his hands together and they made a scruffy sound, as very old wrinkly hands do.

"Pies?" she asked. "I'm having trouble recalling what I do each evening lately. It started when you gave me the herbs."

"They do tend to clear your mind. All for the sake of relaxation, of course," he said. "And yes, you are baking pies, though I've yet to have been offered a piece."

"I haven't seen a pie... I don't recall... there's never any leftover pie, when I get up in the morning," she replied, and then put her hand over her grumbling belly. "But if I ever do, you're more than welcome to a piece."

"That would be lovely," he said, with a twinkle in his eye. "Though you are seeming to be much more... let's say, curvy lately, than your normal string bean self. Maybe you're famished after working in the orchard and then eating the whole pie yourself!"

"It's hard to imagine that," she told him, with an exasperated look in her eye.

He laughed. "I am sure all will make sense in time. Right now, it's most important you continue to get sleep and fertilize your peaches, right?"

"True," she said, running her hands through her hair.

The Orchard Man plucked a peach from a tree and bit into it. "These certainly are fine peaches," he said and grinned, juice dripping from his whiskery chin. "They always make my cheeks blush with color and put a spring in my step."

"No problem," she said. "You do seem to be looking rosy-cheeked these days. Thanks very much for all your advice and herbs. It's the least I can do. Especially if I am tempting you with the smell of pie and not offering you any!"

She chuckled and turned to step inside. She hoped she wasn't eating a whole pie a night, but her pants had been getting a little tighter than normal and there was a time when she ate to her anxiety, but she thought she was coping better getting all that sleep.

Another week went by and one morning, as she fertilized the trees, she realized that she still had the problem of something digging in her orchard. They had raised dirt under at least nine of the peach trees. It didn't seem as if they were digging tunnels or homes though. Could an animal be hoarding food for the winter? There weren't any roaming dogs around, so it must be a woodland creature. She loved animals and didn't want to bring in an exterminator, and so far, they didn't seem to be hurting the trees. By far, the fruit on the peach trees was the best producing and tasting fruit she'd ever grown. She'd rather not mess with what was working. The fertilizer the Orchard Man gave her was making a difference and that's all that mattered.

The missing memories bothered her, even though she was glad to have the herbs to help her drift off to a much more restful sleep. She wasn't as depressed or angry in the mornings either.

She was trying to piece together her evenings each night so she started to keep a journal of what she found each morning to connect the dots. She had even opened the oven, finding sticky peach filling burned to the bottom. The Orchard Man was right, she had indeed been baking pies. Was this causing her chest pains? Was she putting on too much weight from the lard-laden piecrusts?

Though the pain crushed her chest so often and so hard still, she couldn't imagine a few pies over a few weeks would cause so much harm to an otherwise healthy young woman. Would it?

The next day when she saw the Orchard Man, he remarked on her sallow appearance. "Maybe a little of the side effects are settling in from the herbs," he said. "Usually it takes much more time for any to appear, if they do. Some grayness to the skin, dehydration, and tingling in some extremities. I am sorry that I didn't warn you. They are so minor. But it must be worth it to sleep better, right?"

"I suppose so," she said. And really, she did enjoy a good night's sleep. But something was weighing on her mind. When she couldn't put her finger on it, she changed the subject. "So are you selling a lot of seeds for the fall and next spring?"

"Oh, yes, my dear," he said. "Since you let me eat some of your peaches, I am as hearty and joyful as a bluebird, if not as pretty. I haven't felt this good for a while. My bones don't ache, my beard is turning auburn again, and my hair is even growing back! Soon, I'll be dancing jigs like my grand-daddy."

"I'm glad someone is least happy and healthy! You keep eating those peaches."

"Oh, I will, lass, I will," he said, nodding his head. "Your kindness and your peaches restore my soul."

"My pleasure," she said, then turned toward the shed. She had a few things to do around her place to get ready for the approaching autumn months and she liked to get a head start.

She clutched her chest as she walked and hoped she'd be able to finish.

The next week, Mrs. Burk phoned because Melissa hadn't been to the Farmer's After Mart for her eggs. She told of the murder of two more young men. The day after, Melissa had heard the sirens of two police cars swiftly tearing up gravel down the off-the-beaten path that was their country road, and then, through the woods, heard them turn into the driveway of her neighbor on the other side. Though she was ticked off at Mrs. McPherson, the lady didn't know that yet, so she put on airs and gave her a call. She was usually the type of woman who knew everything as soon as it was happening. Melissa, on the other hand, was always in the dark, or with her head in the clouds.

"Do you know what's going on at the neighbors'?" she asked when Mrs. McPherson picked up the phone on the first ring. "I saw the police and..."

"....oh my goodness," Mrs. McPherson cut in. "Mr. and Mrs. Valecourt's son was brutally murdered last night. His heart cut out of his chest! Of all things to happen to someone..." She sobbed on the other end of the receiver.

"Another murder?" Melissa said. "How sad, Mrs. McPherson. Tommy was nice. I know he hung out with... I am sorry to hear it. Are you okay?"

Melissa herself was shaken up, by the murder yes, but also by being reminded of Nic. Tommy was a good kid, but she didn't talk to him anymore, or his parents, as they had sided with Nic, believing whatever story he told them and scorning her. Her hand balled into a fist and her stubby nails pierced into her palm underneath. A soothing mechanism.

"I will be okay, sweetheart," Mrs. McPherson said. "I hope you'll be okay too. This murderer is after boys. Nic will be..."

"Yes... yes, it is," Melissa cut in. "Take care of yourself, Mrs. McPherson."

"We will keep our eyes open even wider now," Mrs. McPherson said. "Once the police are gone, I'll be heading up to the Valencourt's with dinner and a pie. I will give them your condolences."

"Please do," Melissa said, hanging up quickly without saying goodbye.

That night, Melissa went to bed worn and with a headache, hours earlier than normal. She took a sleeping pill from an old prescription. They had made her too groggy in the morning and hadn't done enough good, so she had stopped taking them long ago. However, she was desperate, so with this pill, and a double dose of the herbs from the Orchard Man, she went to bed. She hadn't seen the little man all day, and though she hoped to ask him what he had heard around town about this case, she also hoped she didn't have pie to offer him. She needed to sleep, not bake pies.

When she awoke, it was two days later. Someone pounded on the back door. She sat up, glanced at her hair as she passed by the mirror (noticed that she had some serious bed head), sighed, and stumbled over to pull her soft, white, alpaca wool robe off its hook. Everything in her head was quite fuzzy and the last thing she wanted to do was answer the door. However, the knocking was persistent, and she'd have another headache if she didn't reach the door soon.

When she looked out, she didn't see anyone, even though the incessant knocking continued. She stood back and opened the door. She laughed to herself as she saw the Orchard Man standing there. He was too short to be seen through the window.

Her smile disappeared because he looked so distraught. She immediately knew something was wrong. She squatted down to be face-to-face with him.

"What wrong?" she asked, almost breathlessly. "Are you okay?"

"I've been waiting for you to wake up from this lengthy slumber, but I could wait no longer. I had to warn you."

"Warn me?" she said, becoming alarmed. "What happened, what's going on?" Her chest clenched up tight, so tight that it almost knocked her over.

"You need to run as far as you can go... now," he said. "The police are going to search the wooded areas in this whole strip, and though you feel like you don't have anything to hide, it would behoove you to trust me and run. Don't even take your car and try to go somewhere else. They could follow you, trace you. Just run through the pine trees and to the hills behind them. Quick, put some clothes on."

Melissa went back to the bedroom and threw on her jeans and a Queens of the Stone Age t-shirt. On her way out she grabbed her lightweight, blue sweatshirt off the hook by the back door, deciding not to question the little man she'd come to consider a friend. Even though the pain piercing her heart was overwhelming, her arms almost going numb, she put on her black Converse shoes, tying them quickly. In her backpack, she shoved in a bottle of water and a knife, grabbed from the dish drainer.

The Orchard Man stood, with a concerned look in his eye, and ushered her out the door. "Go, Melissa... hurry," he said.

He waited watching her from the porch, as she ran through the orchard and towards the far tree line, before he trotted off among the knotty peach trees and disappeared.

Melissa scurried through the forest and up and down two hills before she stopped in the farthest grouping of oak trees, a squirrel turning and giving her the once over. She scrambled on the heels of her feet down a steep incline, falling on her butt and hands, and toppled into the ravine. Crawling, groping with her fingers and wrists to steady herself to her feet, she finally fell under the overhang of a large tree, and sat there panting, her chest hurting. She wiped sporadically at the leaves and dirt on her jeans and sweatshirt.

For three nights she sat under the tree, waiting, wondering. She would doze off and on during both the nights and the days, thirsty and confused. As she hadn't taken the herbs with her, she was jolted awake by frightening dreamscape flashes. Was she hallucinating because of such little water and food? In her mind she saw herself murdering these young men. Surely, it was a trick.

By the next night, famished and delirious, her mind had fully realized responsibility for the savage deaths that were occurring. Inconsolable and without understanding of how she could do such acts, and tired of the enormous pain in her own chest, she took the knife from her backpack and impulsively cut out her own heart, screaming at the searing eruption of blood. Alive, though barely, she pulled the organ out of her chest cavity and saw not a beating heart, but a large, petrified stone that looked like pink quartz, carved into the shape of a very large peach pit. She gasped. A second later, it dropped from her hand, as she fell dead in the quiet of the woods, not even a bird above chirping.

The Orchard Man looked up from the newspaper he read at Melissa's kitchen table when he heard the scream. He smiled, and looked back down again to his reading. Happy the cottage was now his home, enacting a spell around the property that would keep people away, no questions asked. The peaches were his key to survival as a human, and more than that, as a young human.

Now that the ground below the trees had been fertilized with the bloody, meaty, feral hearts of young men, the essence of their vitality seeping into the fruit as they blossomed, he could stay comfortably, his immortality made safe. The plan had worked. He rose up and skipped to the stove to put on the teakettle. Atop a stool, he opened the shuttered windows over the sink, breathing in the orchard air.

The crisp, autumn air of his beautiful new orchard.

HARDENED HEARTS

MEETING THE PARENTS

SARAH L. JOHNSON

Mom. Dad. ~~I'd like you to meet my boyfriend, Ned~~
You've asked about this guy I'm seeing and I want you to meet him, I
do, but there's a few things I should
~~He's hairy~~
~~Which can be startling~~
The important thing is that he's got the biggest heart
~~Only one chamber, but it's huge~~
He's a hard worker too. He's in ~~pest control~~
Textiles
Silk, mostly

"Fuck." I ball up the paper and toss it in the bin.

Stuffington peers at me from the top of the bookcase, then retreats into his nap with a rusty feline harrumph. I draw my legs up into my sleep shirt and rest my chin on my knees. I've been at my desk for hours, trying to get something down, and getting precisely nowhere.

Ned's bristly leg rubs against my foot. "Babe, it's okay. I'll just hang out at my place this weekend."

"Absolutely not." I swivel my chair to face him. "I won't keep you hidden away like some nasty secret."

He chuckles. "Is it that big a deal? We're not exactly talking incest and attics."

"You've been reading again."

"The tablet is terrific. So easy to turn the pages."

I reach down and sink my fingers into the coarse hair on his head, stirring up the smell of rain and torn tree bark. A scent that clings to me whenever I touch him.

"Come back to bed," he says.

"I wanted to have something prepared. Something smart, you know?"

He coaxes my legs out of my shirt and my feet onto the floor. When I make no further move to get up, he waits. Then he smiles. Or what I always think of as his smile. His foreleg glides up the inside of my calf, tasting the crease behind my knee. I let my head fall back but feel his eyes on me. All eight of them. A gaze that peels me open every time. I envy his vision.

He crawls up between my legs and rests his head on my stomach. "I know you wouldn't think so, but parents love me."

I believe him. Ned is funny, smart, and kind. A genuinely great guy. Which isn't to say he's perfect, or that he gets along with everyone. My cat, for instance. Stuffington loathes Ned, and the feeling is more than mutual since he ripped off one of Ned's legs. Those things don't grow back overnight. Ned fantasizes about murdering my cat, and while he'd never act on it, he's not above giving Stuffy the odd surprise shower of urticating hairs.

I scrape my fingernails over Ned's carapace. The murmur rumbling through his exoskeleton leaves me wet and wanting as silk threads spin down through our entwined legs and tickle my insteps.

"Why worry about sounding smart when you can just tell them the truth?" he asks.

And the truth is that I'm happy. Ned gets me, in a way no biped ever has. He understands my fear of home ownership and mistrust of people who wear tinted contact lenses. He supports my dreams of cycling through South America and one day opening a yarn store. With him, I listen. With him, I'm heard. I have space. I have intimacy. This is the healthiest relationship I've ever been in.

So what if he bites?

So what if I like it?

Everyone's got kinks.

Not everyone is that open minded. My parents are chill people, but they live in a town where the sidewalks are rolled up at suppertime. I'm in the big bad city getting my well shocked on the reg by a giant arachnid. There's no way to break this to them gently.

"It's not the weirdest thing." His voice is muffled as he dives under the hem of my shirt. "They'll get used to the idea. In the meantime, you need to relax..."

His tarsal claws dig into my hips. Mygalomorphic fangs breach my flesh. I clutch the armrests and whimper as his venom ignites my blood. Shivering and nauseous, I want to pass out even as a rush of pleasure knits me into the pain. From his perch atop the bookcase, Stuffington growls but does not pounce.

```
[9:03pm]<reluctant> Anyone?
[9:03pm]<sexycakes> a/s/l???
[9:03pm]<easypeasy> a/s/l?
[9:04pm]<reluctant> Ummm...
```

MATCHMAKER

MEG ELISON

It's been eight months since she left me.

It's not that long. It still feels fresh. I knew she would get over this faster than me; she was the one who ended it, after all. She knew we were over a long time before I did. Apparently.

But I thought it would be longer before I heard she was back on the market. That happened less than a month after we broke up.

What's that thing where your friends tell you something they think you ought to know, but you were better off not knowing? There should be a word for that. Well-intentioned cruelty.

Maybe all cruelty starts with good intentions.

I wasn't going to look. I managed to make it back to my basement and into my debugging flow for almost two hours before I gave up and pulled out my phone. I've never used a dating app before, so I didn't know that you can't just browse— you have to create a profile before they let you in. I filled out the bare minimum, using a picture of Roger Rabbit and giving one-word answers to every question just to get past the gate. Even after that, it took me a long time to find her. I discarded maybe two hundred girls before she rolled into view.

The picture was new. I heard she cut her hair right after we broke up. She was like a chick flick come to life: dump the guy, chop the hair, laugh over mimosas with friends. But she looked so good, relaxed and happy and ready to start over again.

I'm not just jilted. This is grief. We were together for three years. The last year, she lived with me at my now very empty apartment. She's thinking about dating again and I'm trying to work myself up to selling the ring I bought on eBay.

Her profile makes my heart feel plucked and pincered apart. "Star Wars over Star Trek. Vanilla over chocolate. Dancing over moping. Calzone over pizza. Decisive graphic designer seeks agreeable geek for long arguments about the relative merits of Marvel vs DC vs Dark Horse."

It was like a play-by-play of our first couple of dates. This was the list of things we fell in love over. I guess she thought it would work again.

I wanted to delete the app, but I screenshot her profile on my way out. Just in case I wanted to look again. It might help me sleep.

The afternoon stretched out before me like a tar pit. I tried to go back to work, but I couldn't keep my mind on anything. She left a hole in me so ragged and bloody that I didn't know whether I needed a bandage or a bullet. But I can see now that for her I was like a book slid off the shelf, leaving a neat gap she could just fill with a little online shopping.

Monstrously unfair. I pictured her free and relieved and laughing at the little jokes people made in her inbox as they tried to take her out.

I cried so long in the shower that the water ran cold.

I blocked her, unfollowed her, set up a filter that sent any emails from her address straight to the garbage. Even as I did this, I knew she wouldn't try to contact me. But these were the things I could control.

I asked my friends not to update me on her romantic progress. My friend Matt who works at the Humane Society talked me into adopting a homeless kitten, and slowly I began to feel the torn edges of myself coming back together.

Eight months.

It's a couple orders of magnitude longer than it took her, but at eight months I felt ready. Well, not ready for all of it. Not for the search, and not for the cycle of rejection. Definitely not for some lousy basic survey of all single women near me between twenty-five and thirty-five to bring her grinning face back onto my screen.

I deleted that screenshot. I really am doing better. But just to be sure, I created some rules.

My profile does most of the work: dating sites will only suggest women twenty-five to thirty-five within fifty miles of me who are interested in men. I got a new picture taken where I have a believable smile and enough sleep under my eyes and my kitten (who is now more of a cat) named Heidelberg. I wrote a bio that makes me sound fun rather than desperate. I specified carefully what I am hoping to find.

The rules:

    1. We must have common interests. At least a 50% commonality in basic binary choices expressed by her profile (Marvel over DC, Star Wars over Star Trek, etc). Then, genres, hobbies, causes, and preferences. Simple enough, and most important.

    2. She doesn't have to be a model or anything, but pretty is geometrically quantifiable. I wrote a visual scanning program that maps the face in the profile picture, scoring overall facial symmetry and arrangement of features and proportions against phi. If she's mathematically attractive, she moves on.

3. She should be as little like my ex as possible. This is a tricky one. My ex and I shared a lot of common interests obviously, so this rule can't interfere with #1. (Behold Asimov as Cupid.) My ex was beautiful, so this rule has to be subordinate to #2. However, any prospective date cannot share online friends with her, work in a similar field, come from the same town, or have the same name. Even variants of it still set loose bats in my ribcage.

After building profiles for every viable dating site (no simple undertaking) I created a bot that waits for all these criteria to be filled. If these scripts return a success, the bot chooses a time and date that I'm free, picks a restaurant or a bar I've been to and rated four stars or better, and then triggers the sending of a pre-written message (the script quits after two messages a week; I'm only one man.) The message template's fields are populated with the girl's name, the details of the date I'm offering, and a dumb joke at the end.

None of these sites have an API that allows me to automate this process, naturally. This is a careful series of idempotent operations, with human-like pauses between them, all slow and strictly sequential, ordered so that each success initiates the next part of the process or halts it, killing the process if it returns a bad result.

The bot does not notify me unless I receive a reply, and the reply does not include rejection, non-match, or kill words/phrases (creep, no thank you, gross, etc). I think I've outlined those thoroughly enough.

This takes me a week of evenings to engineer. The process is intricate enough that I lose myself in the work and I can distance myself from the dissociative prospect of advertising myself as a mate in a saturated market while risking spending the rest of my life alone with this cat. I like Heidelberg a lot, sometimes I wake up and find a tiny paw in my curled hand and feel a gratitude I could drown in. But loneliness is a particular bug; a cronjob that never stops firing even when I sleep. It will not settle for cats.

Once I know the daemons are running and successfully test the system, I don't think about it. I feel accomplished. I'm doing the work of finding a partner without the drag of repetition or the stab of getting shut down. I'm not bothering anyone with unwanted advances or adding my voice to the cacophony of guys trying to get laid with quotes from books they read in high school.

I put it out of my mind. I focus on work, I go to the gym, I hang out with my friends and I am really laughing with them again, not just mirroring so that they'll believe I'm all right.

Matt's girlfriend Anya lets it slip over drinks that my ex is moving in with her new guy. I feel a twinge, but it's small. From here, it seems like we were always going to end up apart. I smile. It's a little one, but genuine. I really do hope she's happy.

And at just that moment, an achievement unlocked: I get a push notification from my bot.

The bot schedules the date for Friday night at seven at my favorite bar by accessing my check-in history and interfacing with my mostly-empty Google calendar. The bar features a moose head with Mardi Gras beads dripping off its antlers above the door, and they make gimlets right in front of you out of fresh limes. I tell her I'll be wearing a peacoat. She answers back immediately that she'll see me there.

I try to make myself work until 18:30 but I can't sit still. In her profile picture, she looks like tinsel and confetti and sprinkles and other things that make something nice just a little bit nicer. Her bio has a pun and some buried references to Dr. Who. Even if we don't hit it off, she's the kind of woman I'd like to be friends with.

So I head out at 18:00, to get one gimlet ahead and find a seat where I can watch the door.

There's snow in her hair when she walks in. It must have just started. She smiles a little when she sees me, but she gets her own gimlet on her way to the table. She looks nervous.

I stand, but she waves me and my outdated gestures away. I like the sound of her name. She gulps her drink and looks at me like she's checking for horns.

"I'm really glad you came."

She laughs nervously and looks away from me. "I wasn't sure about it at all. The minute I stepped outside it started to snow. I hope it doesn't pile up too much before we head out."

"It's no big deal, I brought my skis." I bring up one of my enormous feet, size fifteen and freaky narrow. "My mom called them my skis when I was a kid. Growth spurts had me looking like a stick figure."

She laughs again, easier this time and points at my foot. "That's unreal! I could go kayaking in one of those shoes!"

We both relax a bit. We get another round. We find a wavelength. It's going pretty well. I remember that this part can be fun as well as terrifying. I catch her sneaking glances when I'm looking away. I haven't smiled this much in a long time and my face hurts a little.

She talks too fast, like she's confessing, and my face relaxes into a small O as she begins to explain.

"Listen, this is going to sound weird. But I have to tell you, I don't really use dating sites. I just created a bot that does the work for me, and then notifies me when I get a message that actually proposes a date and doesn't have a dick pic attached. I created some simple rules—"

I burst out laughing.

Another eight months goes by. Kittens become cats. Dates become all the time. Together, we write one more script.

```
(deftype Partner
  GoodTimes
    (enjoy [this ^Partner them]
      (>! them (best-of this))
      (integrate! this (<! them)))
  BadTimes
    (deal-with [this that ^Partner them]
      (let [the-rest (deal! that can-deal?)]
        (>! them the-rest)
        (when-let [more (<! them)]
          (deal-with this more them)))
      (sustain! this (<! them)))))

  (defn life [today me you]
    (cons (live! today me you)
          (lazy-seq (life (<! @WHAT_COMES) you
me))))
```

Somewhere, Asimov cocks his bow.

CONTRIBUTORS

Gwendolyn Kiste

Gwendolyn Kiste is the author of *And Her Smile Will Untether the Universe*, her debut fiction collection from JournalStone, as well as the dark fantasy novella, *Pretty Marys All in a Row*, from Broken Eye Books. Her short fiction has appeared in Nightmare Magazine, Shimmer, Black Static, Daily Science Fiction, Interzone, LampLight, and Three-Lobed Burning Eye, among others. You can find her online at gwendolynkiste.com.

Somer Canon

Somer Canon is a minivan revving suburban mother who avoids her neighbors for fear of being found out as a weirdo. When she's not peering out of her windows, she's consuming books, movies, and video games that sate her need for blood, gore, and things that disturb her mother.

Calvin Demmer

Calvin Demmer is a dark fiction author. His work has appeared in Broadswords and Blasters, Empyreome Magazine, Mad Scientist Journal, Ravenwood Quarterly, Switchblade, and others. When not writing, he is intrigued by that which goes bump in the night and the sciences of our universe. You can find him online at www.calvindemmer.com.

Theresa Braun

Theresa Braun was born in St. Paul, Minnesota and has carried some of that hardiness with her to South Florida where she currently resides. Traveling, ghost hunting, and all things dark are her passions. Her stories appear in The Horror Zine, Schlock! Webzine, and Sirens Call, among others; upcoming stories will be published in Bards and Sages and Strange Behaviors. Twitter: @tbraun_author; website: www.theresabraun.com.

John Boden
John Boden lives in the wilds of central Pa, with his wife and sons. A baker by day, he writes unique fiction in whatever time is left. His work has received kind words of praise from some.

Tom Deady
Tom Deady's novel, *Haven*, won the 2016 Bram Stoker Award for Superior Achievement in a First Novel. His short stories have appeared in several anthologies and he released his second novel, *Eternal Darkness* and a novella, *Weekend Getaway*, in 2017. Tom also has a Young Adult series he is seeking agent representation for. He resides in Massachusetts where he is working on his next novel.

J.L. Knight
J.L. Knight lives in Kentucky and works at an antiquarian bookstore that is probably haunted.

Madhvi Ramani
Madhvi Ramani grew up in London. She writes short fiction, articles, essays, children's books, and drama. Her work has been published by the BBC, Asia Literary Review, Stand Magazine and others. She currently lives a thoroughly bohemian lifestyle in Berlin. Find out more @ www.madhviramani.com or follow her on Twitter @madhviramani.

Scott Hallam

Scott Paul Hallam is a short story author living in Pittsburgh, PA. His work has been published in Cease, Cows and Night to Dawn magazine. He earned his Master's in English Literature from Duquesne University and first fell in love with the written word when his dad would read him stories by Edgar Allan Poe as a kid. You can follow him on Twitter at @ScottHallam1313.

Robert Dean

Robert Dean is a writer, journalist, and cynic. His most recent novel, The Red Seven was called "rich in vivid imagery, quirky characterizations, and no holds barred violence and mayhem. I never knew what the word romp really meant until now, but in case you're wondering, this is it" by Shotgun Logic.

His essays have been featured in Jackson Free Press, Victoria Advocate, and The Austin American Statesman. He's also been on NPR.

Robert is finishing a New Orleans-based crime thriller called A Hard Roll. He lives in Austin and likes ice cream and koalas. Stalk him on Twitter: @Robert_Dean.

Leo X. Robertson

Leo X. Robertson is a Scottish process engineer and writer, currently living in Oslo, Norway. He has work most recently published by Helios Quarterly, Unnerving Magazine, Expanded Horizons and Open Pen, among others. His novella, *The Grimhaven Disaster*, was released by Unnerving earlier this year. Find him on Twitter @Leoxwrite or check out his website: leoxrobertson.wordpress.com.

Jennifer Williams

Jennifer Williams is an author, editor, cat lady and coffee enthusiast. Her fiction has previously appeared in *Women of the Bite: Lesbian Vampire Erotica* edited by Cecilia Tan, *Vicious Verses and Reanimated Rhymes*, a collection of zombie poetry edited by A.P. Fuchs, and most recently in A Tribute Anthology to Deadworld and Comic Publisher Gary Reed edited by Lori Perkins. You can find her on Twitter at @JenWilliams13.

Erin Sweet Al-Mehairi

Erin Al-Mehairi is the author of *Breathe. Breathe.*, a collection of dark fiction featuring short stories and poetry, also published by Unnerving. She is a marketing and public relations professional, journalist, and editor of over 20 years and lives in rural Ohio. You can hear her #marketingmorsels segment on The Mando Method podcast on Project Entertainment Network, and besides on all the other social media outlets, you can find her on her blog at www.hookofabook.wordpress.com.

Sarah L. Johnson

Sarah L. Johnson lives in Calgary where she's mastered the art of the writerly side hustle, working in a bookstore, teaching creative writing, and freelance editing. Her short story collection *Suicide Stitch* (EMP Publishing) was published in 2015 and her debut novel *Infractus* will be released in April 2018 by Coffin Hop Press.

Meg Elison

Meg Elison is a science fiction author and feminist essayist. Her debut novel, *The Book of the Unnamed Midwife*, won the

2014 Philip K. Dick Award. She has been published in McSweeney's, Fantasy & Science Fiction, Catapult, and many other places. Elison is a high school dropout and a graduate of UC Berkeley.

James Newman

James Newman is the author of the novels *Midnight Rain, The Wicked, Animosity*, and *Ugly as Sin*, the collection *People are Strange*, and the critically-acclaimed novella *Odd Man Out*. Up next are the novels *Dog Day o' Summer* and *Scapegoat* (co-written with Mark Allan Gunnells and Adam Howe, respectively).

Eddie Generous

Eddie Generous is the creator, editor, designer, and publisher of Unnerving and Unnerving Magazine. In early 2018, Hellbound Books is publishing a collection of his novelettes titled *Dead is Dead, but Not Always*, and also in 2018 he is teaming up with Mark Allan Gunnells and Renee Miller to release *Splish, Slash, Takin' a Bloodbath*, a collection of short stories.

Made in the USA
Lexington, KY
14 March 2018